ALONE IN THE CROWD

"I have a feeling that the girl is who wrote this song is really intense—really terrific," Guy said softly to Lynne, his brown eyes shining. "I can just tell by listening to her that she's not like anybody else around here. Playing backups for her would be like a dream come true. Like playing for Linda Ronstadt," he added, smiling at her.

Lynne felt her mouth go dry. Guy probably thought this girl looked like Linda Ronstadt, too.

Someone terrific, he had said. Lynne didn't have to think too hard to imagine what *that* meant. Someone curvy, lithe, beautiful, someone who would look as good onstage as she sounded.

How right she'd been to keep her song anonymous! Lynne couldn't bear disappointing Guy, dashing his dream to bits. Let him keep thinking this anonymous songwriter was the girl he had been waiting for all his life.

Lynne knew better, and she was determined no one else would learn the truth, however hard it became to keep her identity a secret.

Bantam Books in the Sweet Valley High Series
Ask your bookseller for the books you have missed

SWEET VALLEY HIGH

ALONE IN THE CROWD

Written by
Kate William

Created by
FRANCINE PASCAL

BANTAM BOOKS
TORONTO · NEW YORK · LONDON · SYDNEY · AUCKLAND

RL 6, IL age 12 and up

ALONE IN THE CROWD
A Bantam Book / May 1986

Sweet Valley High is a trademark of Francine Pascal

Conceived by Francine Pascal

Produced by Cloverdale Press, Inc.

Cover art by James Mathewuse

ISBN 0-553-26825-2

Published simultaneously in the United States and Canada

Bantam Books are published by Bantam Books, Inc. Its trademark, consisting
of the words "Bantam Books" and the portrayal of a rooster, is Registered in
U.S. Patent and Trademark Office and in other countries. Marca Registrada.
Bantam Books, Inc., 666 Fifth Avenue, New York, New York 10103.

PRINTED IN THE UNITED STATES OF AMERICA

O   13 12 11 10 9 8 7 6 5

ALONE IN THE CROWD

One

"Listen, you guys!" Jessica Wakefield said, her blue-green eyes flashing with excitement as she jumped to her feet and pushed her chair back from the crowded lunch table. "I've finally come up with the perfect way to raise money for the cheerleaders. It's so perfect, it's going to make history around here!"

"Don't talk about making history," Winston Egbert said and groaned. The tall, lanky boy was generally known as the clown of the junior class at Sweet Valley High and was always ready with a joke. "I've got a test in Fellows's class right after lunch," he went on, pretending to tear his dark hair out. "So if you're going to make history, Jess, make it soon. I need to learn some history good and fast!"

Everyone at the table groaned.

"What's your idea, Jess?" Elizabeth asked from across the table, flashing her sister a smile. Watching her twin glow with inspiration was like watching a light blub brighten. Though years of experience had taught Elizabeth that her sister was too often carried away, letting her enthusiasm and high spirits get her into trouble, she still found Jessica's excitement infectious.

It was funny, she thought now, watching Jessica's face light up, as she prepared to explain her idea to the table of classmates looking expectantly up at her. As far as appearances went, she and her twin were mirror images. But when it came to their personalities, it was difficult to believe they were related!

Sixteen years old, the twins were both model-slim, with gleaming blond hair, streaked by the California sun, and wide-set eyes that were the blue-green color of the Pacific Ocean. But Elizabeth's eyes were like the Pacific on a calm, serene day. As for Jessica—her eyes were more often stormy and flashing. Though Elizabeth was only four minutes older than her twin, she often felt the gap was more like four years. Jessica was so impulsive, so impractical! Elizabeth thought. She fell in and out of love at the wink of an eye, much to the dismay of her crowd of admirers, and her interest in her hobbies was equally passionate and short-lived. She would throw herself into something, such as gourmet cooking, and a few weeks later she would forget all about it. Elizabeth, on the other hand, knew exactly what she wanted to devote her spare time to: writing. That was why she spent long hours after school, working on *The Oracle*, the school newspaper, for which she wrote the "Eyes and Ears" column, keeping her classmates abreast of the latest gossip at Sweet Valley High.

"We need something really different," Jessica was saying now, tossing her silky hair off her shoulder. "That's what we said at our last meeting. Only no one could come up with anything special."

"That's right," Cara Walker chimed in, her brown eyes thoughtful. Pretty, dark-haired Cara was on the cheerleading squad with Jessica. "And we're really desperate for money," she added. "We've *got* to get new uniforms. The ones we've been wearing are almost in rags!"

"You can say that again," Lila Fowler agreed, making a face as she pushed her light brown hair back from her face.

"How about the Fowler Fund for Uniform Rehabilitation?" Winston cracked slyly.

Lila glared at him. She hated being teased about the fact that her father was one of the wealthiest men in Southern California. "This is serious, Winston," she said coldly. "You don't have to be rude. Besides," she added with a pout, "I'm sure Daddy would say that the

3

cheerleaders should work for the money. He says it builds character."

Elizabeth could barely suppress a giggle, especially when she saw the expression on Enid Rollins's face—a cross between a grimace and a smirk. Enid was Elizabeth's dearest friend and confidante, and Elizabeth knew that Enid was probably thinking that Lila had never done a day's work in her life.

"So what's your idea, Jess?" Cara cut in. "I hope it's good. You're sure giving it a big buildup."

"Well, what do you think of this?" Jessica said dramatically, stepping back from the table and spreading out her arms as if to present an imaginary spectacle. "A rocking chair relay in the gym. Each girl on the squad will take turns rocking, and we'll sign up pledges in advance for every thirty minutes we rock. It'll be a scream, the most original fund-raising event in years!"

Cara frowned. "*Rocking* chairs? Jess, I think *you're* off your rocker! It's so"—she paused, thinking—"peculiar!"

"Don't be a spoilsport," Jessica reproached her. "It'll be great! We can use my parents' big old rocking chair. We'll take turns rocking, and the others can"—she thought for a few moments—"have a good time at the party that'll be going on at the same time!" she said triumphantly.

4

"What sort of party?" Enid asked, intrigued.

"We'll call it the Rock Around the Clock relay!" Jessica exclaimed, her eyes twinkling. "Maybe we can get The Droids to play for us, too. It'll be just like a school dance, only a million times better!"

Winston pretended to collapse on the table. "Give us a break, Jess. We just got through with that blowout picnic of yours. We need some rest!"

Jessica laughed. Winston was referring to the picnic she had organized as part of the recent Sweet Valley Centennial Celebration. The entire celebration had been a smashing success, and Jessica was proud of how well the picnic had turned out.

"I think the relay's a great idea," Elizabeth said loyally. "It sure is original. Besides, I'll bet The Droids would be happy for an excuse to make a big appearance soon. Did you hear they're going to announce a contest to find a new hit song?"

Enid's eyebrows lifted. The Droids were one of the most popular young bands in the area. Although they were still only juniors in high school, they had received a good deal of attention.

"I heard Guy Chesney talking about that," Jessica said, plopping down in her chair again and taking a bite out of her apple. "He said he wants to find something new—kind of a signature song. He said a great song can make a band!"

"That's for sure," Enid said. "A good song can be all it takes."

"So when's this big Rock Around the Clock relay supposed to take place?" Winston demanded, putting down his notebook.

Jessica sniffed. "None of you seems very interested," she said sulkily. "If I can't even get any support from my very own friends—my very own *squadmates*," she added, frowning at Cara.

"Jess, it's a marvelous idea," Elizabeth said warmly. "You can count on all of us to pledge money. Right, guys?"

"Right!" everyone chimed in.

Jessica looked mollified. "I was thinking we should try to have it soon. We need the money right away, and if everyone on the squad gets going, I don't see why we can't have it next weekend. How does a week from Saturday night sound?"

Elizabeth laughed. Seeing her sister's organizational tactics at work was always interesting. "Why are you asking us?" she demanded. "Don't you think you'd better ask The Droids and check with the office about using the gym?"

"Good point!" Jessica exclaimed, jumping to her feet again. "I'm so lucky to have a genius for a twin!" The next minute she was off, dashing

6

away in such a hurry that she almost smashed into a girl who was walking slowly toward her, head lowered. "Watch out!" Jessica exclaimed, shaking her head in irritation as she headed off in the direction of the office.

"Liz, what's that girl's name?" Enid asked in a low voice, leaning forward to get a better look as the girl lifted her head, gazed about her with a look of confusion and unhappiness, then lowered her head again, and walked slowly to a table.

"Her name is Sherry, isn't it?" Winston asked.

"What an unfortunate outfit she has on, whoever she is," Lila commented with a yawn.

Elizabeth frowned. "It isn't Sherry," she said. "It's Lynne Henry. She's kind of quiet," she added. Recently Elizabeth had been noticing the tall, reclusive junior and wondering what she was like.

"Lynne Henry!" Enid exclaimed, snapping her fingers. "I keep seeing her around, but I couldn't remember her name. She's in two of my classes, but she never says a word. She's like a ghost or something. She just kind of drifts in at the last minute, sits really quietly in her seat, and leaves when the bell rings. She never talks to *anyone*."

"I don't think she has any friends," Elizabeth said sadly.

"She doesn't look very appealing," Lila said

disparagingly. "I can't imagine who would want to be friends with someone like *her*."

"Lila," Winston chided her, "haven't you got a single kind bone in your whole body?"

Lila grimaced. "*Look* at her, though. She's just sitting there, staring at her sandwich like she's in another world or something."

Elizabeth turned to follow Lila's gaze. Sure enough, Lynne Henry was sitting alone, elbows propped up on the empty table, her face expressionless.

Elizabeth felt a tiny shiver go through her. "She must be lonely," she said softly, watching the girl take a bite of her sandwich and chew it automatically, as if she couldn't even taste it. Elizabeth couldn't imagine eating lunch by herself, sitting alone in the crowded lunchroom while everyone else talked and laughed.

The girl's expression looked so unwelcoming, though, so stony. Elizabeth wondered what she was thinking. Sighing, Elizabeth turned back to her friends, her eyes thoughtful.

But she only half-heard what Winston was saying about his history test. She was wondering about Lynne Henry.

The thing is, Lynne was telling herself, *I just have to act as if I don't care. If I can tell myself that, everything's going to be OK.*

She hated lunchtime. The rest of the day was

8

all right—not spectacular, but not terrible, either. She had gotten so used to the routine at school that she could practically get through the day as if she were sleepwalking. And sometimes that was what it felt like, too.

But lunchtime was awful. She felt self-conscious getting into the cafeteria line by herself. Everyone else waited for friends, joked around, made conversation. Nobody said anything to Lynne, though. She might as well have been invisible.

Lynne had opened the brown lunch bag her mother had packed for her and automatically unwrapped the sandwich. She had taken a bite, telling herself the sooner she finished it, the quicker she could go back to the library. If the librarians would have let her, she would have eaten lunch there. But food was forbidden in the library. "Lunchtime is supposed to be relaxing," the head librarian had told her once with a smile. "Why don't you go meet some of your friends?"

And what was I supposed to say to that? Lynne thought miserably, putting her sandwich down with a frown. *That I don't have any friends? That I'm a total nobody?*

Until Lynne had started high school, she hadn't really believed that. She had told herself things would get better when she was a little older, when people stopped caring so much about who was pretty, who was in with the "right" crowd, all that.

But now that Lynne was a junior, she didn't have any delusions any more. People didn't want to be friends with her. They didn't even notice she existed! She just kind of faded into the background.

Picking her sandwich up again, Lynne remembered the day the week before in her English class when Mr. Collins had read a poem out loud. She liked English, and she liked Mr. Collins. He looked like a movie star. He had reddish-blond hair and a warm smile, and he was really young. Everyone liked him. But more important, he had actually complimented Lynne several times, writing nice things at the end of the compositions she wrote. Once he had written that she seemed to have a natural flair for writing. That had made her glow for days. If only he knew how much that meant to her!

But she still got a bad taste in her mouth when she remembered the sound of Mr. Collins's voice, reading the Emily Dickinson poem out loud:

"I'm nobody! Who are you?
Are you nobody, too?"

She had sat up with a start, shaken out of her daydream, her heart pounding. "I'm nobody! Who are you?" It was as if Mr. Collins had found

10

her diary and read it out loud. She could have written those lines. It was as if her own inner voice were speaking!

Mr. Collins had continued to read, his rich voice bringing the poem to life. Then he had put the book down and asked the students what they thought of the poem. And one by one, hands had gone up. Opinions were voiced. Lynne had just sat there, praying the bell would ring. She had never felt so terrible before. *I'm nobody*, she kept thinking. What a depressing thing to say. How could Emily Dickinson have written that?

She hadn't heard anything else Mr. Collins said. She was daydreaming again, imagining she was upstairs in her bedroom at home, with the door closed, playing her guitar. She could practically feel the strings under her fingers. Lynne adored the guitar. When she played, she didn't feel like a nobody.

But there was still the rest of the lunch hour to get through and the rest of the long, dragging afternoon before she could get on the bus and go home. Lynne put her sandwich down again, her eyes filling with tears.

"Lynne!" a male voice called, interrupting her reverie.

Lynne's eyes widened in disbelief, her heart beginning to hammer. Turning around, she saw Keith Webster, the good-looking forward on the basketball team, waving frantically across the room. At *her?* Her mouth dry, she started to get to her feet.

"I'm coming, silly!" a high-pitched voice behind her called back, and Lynne Jacobs, a sophomore with shiny black hair and a glowing complexion, raced across the cafeteria and linked arms with Keith.

Lynne sank back down into her chair, the color draining from her face. She didn't know why she had kidded herself that way. She wasn't Lynne. She was nobody.

Two

The crowd waiting for the bus after school seemed even more animated than usual. It seemed that way to Lynne, anyway, who was standing off by herself, her backpack slung over one shoulder, her eyes on the pavement.

"Dance with me, Caroline!" Winston Egbert crooned, stepping gallantly forward and greeting Caroline Pearce with a mock bow. The redhead burst into giggles.

"You're too much, Winston," she said merrily, clearly loving the attention.

"I'm serious," Winston protested. "Let's do the I'm-waiting-for-the-bus two-step. It's one of my favorites."

Still giggling, Caroline took Winston's hand, and the two made a halfhearted attempt to repeat the steps they had learned in ballroom dancing the year before. They were both laughing.

The crowd began cheering. "That Winston," a sophomore girl said, grabbing her boyfriend by the hand.

"Madam, your golden chariot approacheth," Winston was saying to Caroline, bowing again and pointing to the yellow school bus.

Lynne's heart began to pound. It was so stupid to make a big deal out of something as ordinary as a bus ride home. But she hated riding the bus. It seemed as if everyone else had someone to sit with. It reminded her of the game they used to play when they were kids. When the music stopped playing, everyone grabbed a place to sit. Everyone, that was, but the loser. The odd man out.

Or in this case, the odd *girl* out. From now on, Lynne decided suddenly, she was going to walk to school. She couldn't stand this anymore.

Soon the bus was filled with chattering, laughing students. Sighing, Lynne sat down next to the window, her backpack on her lap. *Just ten more minutes*, she told herself. Then she would be home, and another long day would be safely behind her.

Lynne barely noticed when Caroline sank down in the seat next to her, her arms spilling over with books and papers. Lynne was staring out the window, her brow wrinkling with concentration. Sometimes, even on a crowded, noisy bus, Lynne could concentrate so hard that she could hear music in her head. Not music she knew, but the start of something, a new song. It was her secret, and it made it easier to be alone. If people knew, they would probably laugh at her, she thought uneasily. But no one was going to find out.

Ever since she was a little girl Lynne Henry had dreamed of one thing, and one thing only: becoming a famous songwriter. When she was a kid, she was always begging her mother to let her take music lessons. She was always humming to herself, making up little songs when she was in the bathtub or taking a walk. She loved to sing. And her voice teacher said she had talent! When she was young, Lynne had wanted to be a performer as well as a songwriter. She had dreamed of being up on a huge stage, belting out song after song, dazzling the audience.

But as Lynne grew older, she realized she wasn't ever going to get up on any stage. And no one was going to applaud her performance, either. It was one thing to fantasize when she was a kid, an ugly duckling. But *this* duckling had never turned into a swan, she reminded herself grimly. Just an ugly duck. And who wanted to pay to see an ugly duck on stage?

Lynne knew she wasn't kidding herself. She was just being objective. Every time she looked in the mirror, she felt like crying. Everything about her was so *plain*—plain light brown, kinky hair. A blah-looking complexion. Her nose was a shade too long, her chin a touch too prominent. When all the other girls had filled out in seventh or eighth grade, getting curves in the right places, Lynne had just gotten taller and thinner. She towered over most of the girls in her class, which always made her feel like some kind of freak. No wonder she slumped. Her mother was forever telling her to stand up straight, as if there were nothing wrong with being five foot ten in her stocking feet.

Lynne heaved an enormous sigh as the bus lurched out of the parking lot. She was thinking that it was easy for her mother to talk. Her mother was tall, too, but she also happened to be breathtakingly beautiful—slender, graceful, with silky black hair always cut in the most glamorous current style. It was just too depressing for words. To make matters worse, her mother had made a career out of glamour. She was the manager of the Silver Door, an elegant health club in a neighboring town. Day after day, Jade Henry dealt in beauty—creams, lotions, exercise equipment, saunas, make-overs.

Lynne knew her mother was disappointed in her. Who could blame her? Jade Henry had everything: wit, charm, good looks, a million friends. How could she help but wish her daughter were a little more like her?

Lynne had inherited only one trait from her glamorous mother: her almond-shaped, gold-flecked green eyes. Unfortunately Lynne was nearsighted, so her beautiful eyes were barely visible behind her thick glasses. "Get contact lenses," her mother had kept urging her, and finally she had given in. But she felt too self-conscious to wear the lenses. She was certain everyone would laugh at her if she wore them to school. They would think she was fooling herself, trying to look *good* or something. So nobody noticed that Lynne had beautiful eyes.

Mrs. Henry's friends all said the same thing— that Lynne looked exactly like her father. And *that*, Lynne thought moodily, still staring out the window, was clearly the kiss of death. Max Henry may have been a lot of things—clever, enterprising, ambitious—but when it came to the looks department, he wasn't much. Her mother had said as much.

Lynne could barely remember her father. He had died when she was three. Sometimes, when she closed her eyes and concentrated really, really hard, she could remember hanging onto him, her little arms around his neck, while he sang to her. But she couldn't really remember his face. She had seen pictures, of course. And there was no denying it: she was Daddy's girl. Unruly hair, prominent chin, sallow complexion—the works!

Still, Lynne knew she had gotten something else from her father, too. Though her mother didn't talk about him much, Lynne had overheard her telling a friend once that he had dreamed of being a musician before they got married. Having a wife and baby to support, he had given music up, taking a job in an insurance company. "But he kept fooling around with his saxophone," Lynne had heard her mother say. "He loved music."

Maybe that was why Lynne felt so shy about her music around her mother. True, she had always begged for lessons. But the older she got, the harder it was to play in front of her mother. It seemed as if the magic disappeared the minute anyone else was around. Lynne hadn't even told her mother that she had gotten a job teaching guitar at the Music Center on Saturday mornings. It was her secret, and it was going to stay that way!

With a start, Lynne realized that the bus was approaching her stop. She chided herself for being so absentminded and awkwardly got to her feet when the driver opened the door a moment later. "Excuse me," she said to Caroline, pushing woodenly past her.

The bus stop was a five-minute walk from Lynne's house, and after she had adjusted her backpack, she set out with a feeling of relief. The ordeal was over; she was almost home. She was just beginning to hum the few bars of the song she had been working on when she saw someone who made the breath catch in her throat. It was *him*: Guy Chesney, the keyboard player for The Droids. Lynne flushed right up to the roots of her hair.

Two weeks earlier, Lynne had watched Guy and The Droids perform at the Sweet Valley Centennial student picnic. Something had made Lynne inexplicably happy that day. Perhaps it was the beautiful sunny weather or the cheerful mood that pervaded the crowd celebrating the hundredth anniversary of the town's founding. Whatever it was, for the first time Lynne started to feel as though she belonged somewhere. But then The Droids began to play a love song. At that moment Lynne looked around her at the smiling faces of the crowd, and a wave of loneliness washed over her. As hard as Lynne tried to force away her despair, she felt herself being overcome. Instead of feeling part of the celebration, Lynne felt like an outsider who was watching the festivities but had no real part in them. Tears began to fall from her eyes, and Lynne found herself turning away from the bandstand and running away from the picnic, away from all of those happy people who made her feel so alone.

"Hi," Guy said, falling into step beside her, looking at her with a faintly quizzical expression on his face.

Lynne couldn't believe how cute he was up close. Her heart thumped wildly.

Lynne knew Guy had moved into her neighborhood a few months before, and sometimes she saw him walking to or from school when she looked out the bus window. He must have left school earlier than usual that day to have gotten this far so fast.

"You're Lynne, right?" he was saying, smiling at her. "I've seen you around at school, but I don't think we've ever met."

"Uh—yes, my name is Lynne Henry," she said, all in a rush.

He was smiling apologetically. "I really don't get to see very many people these days. The Droids and my parents—that's about it!"

"It must be so wonderful," Lynne burst out, "playing with a group like The Droids!"

Guy looked surprised. "Not many people feel that way," he said. "Not many girls, anyway. Most girls I know think music is OK as long as it stays in the background. But playing in a band . . ."

"I think it's exciting," Lynne said vehemently. "What kind of music do you listen to when you're not practicing?"

She couldn't believe how easy it was to talk to

him. He was so easygoing, so relaxed. He was listing bands to her—many of them her own favorites—and in no time at all, they had reached her front walk.

"What about female vocalists?" Lynne asked shyly, hating to end the conversation.

Guy looked thoughtful. "You know, I like some of the mellow stuff. Linda Ronstadt was my favorite the whole time I was growing up."

"I think she's great, too!" Lynne said enthusiastically.

"You do?" Guy beamed. The next minute he was rattling off all the things he liked about the singer: the richness of her voice, her lyrics, her range. Lynne just listened, enthralled. Guy really seemed eager to talk about music, she thought. She barely said a word, and yet, several minutes later, he seemed to mean it when he said it had been good talking to her.

As she watched him walk away, she hoped she would run into him again—and soon.

Humming to herself, Lynne unlocked the front door and let herself inside. The Henrys' tidy front room was filled with amaryllis, her mother's favorite, amaryllis. Lynne barely noticed the flowers as she tossed her jacket over the banister and strolled into the kitchen to fix herself a snack. She loved this time of day. Her mother wouldn't be home for another hour and a half, and Lynne had the house to herself. It was so peaceful. All day she'd dreamed of this. Finally, finally, she was home.

But Lynne didn't feel quite as glad as usual for the anticipated peace and quiet. Taking a sandwich upstairs, she wondered what it was that felt different that day. The small house looked exactly the way it always did, the sleek, handsome furniture, the rich Oriental rugs, and tasteful art creating a subdued, elegant effect.

Lynne closed her door behind her and took a bite of her sandwich. Her gaze ran around her room. Everything was just as she had left it that morning, her canopy bed neatly made, her curtains rustling slightly in front of the open window. Setting her plate down on her desk, Lynne sank down on the side of her bed, picked up her guitar, and cradled it in her arms. Then she tried an experimental chord.

But the song she had been working on wouldn't come. Lynne sat quietly for a minute, trying to concentrate.

She knew now what felt different. There wasn't anything different about the house; *she* felt different. She couldn't stop thinking about Guy Chesney, and the way his eyes crinkled up at the corners when he smiled.

Lynne tried another chord, waiting for the music to pull her back into her familiar, solitary world. Instead, every chord, every bar, every note reminded her of him.

"Guy," she said aloud, a flush coming to her cheeks as she pronounced his name for the first time.

Three

"Lynne!" Mrs. Henry called, her voice high with annoyance. "I've been calling you for the last ten minutes. Do you have any idea what time it is?"

Lynne sat up, rubbing her eyes and blinking in confusion at her alarm clock. "I must've turned it off and fallen back asleep," she mumbled, groping for her glasses.

"It's almost eight o'clock!" her mother added. She opened the door to her daughter's bedroom and frowned at Lynne. "I don't understand how a healthy teenager can sleep as much as you do."

Lynne sighed. "I didn't go to bed until after midnight, Mom. I was working on—" She bit her lip. She didn't want to tell her mother what she had been doing. Actually, she'd been working on a song the previous night, and once she got started, she couldn't stop. But her mother wouldn't understand. Everything *she* did was on schedule. Looking at her mother right now, Lynne wondered how on earth they could even be related. Her mother looked absolutely stunning in a pair of crisp white cotton jeans and a black silk T-shirt. Lynne couldn't imagine owning anything white. She was so messy she knew it would be ruined the minute she put it on!

"Why don't you get dressed?" her mother was saying, opening the curtains to let the early morning sun stream in. "I've got breakfast ready."

"OK," Lynne said, hopping out of bed and grabbing the sweatshirt robe she'd rescued from the box her mother had been about to send to the Salvation Army. "I'll be down in a second."

Lynne knew from experience that her mother's frown meant she was fighting for control. *She probably wants to tell me to take some time with my appearance,* Lynne thought, grabbing the rolled-up pair of jeans she'd thrown on the floor the night before and heading for the bathroom that adjoined her bedroom. But Lynne had given up on her appearance. A quick shower and a tug-of-war with her hairbrush was about all she could handle. She pulled her jeans on, noticing absentmindedly that they really *were* kind of baggy, and went back to her closet, grabbing the first sweatshirt she saw. It was dark green and said Ohio State on the front. Lynne loved sweatshirts. She knew no one could tell she had a figure under this kind of clothing, but that was the idea. Who'd want to look at a tall, spindly body like hers, anyway?

Lynne looked at herself in the full-length mirror her mother had installed in her closet. "Pathetic," she told herself, pushing her glasses up higher on her nose and shaking her head from side to side. "Truly pathetic. Lynne Henry, you are too ugly to be human."

"Lynne!" her mother called. "I've got to leave for work soon, and I want to talk to you!"

Uh-oh, Lynne thought, grabbing her notebook and reading through the words she had finally settled on the previous night before she'd fallen asleep. The song was called "Thinking of Him." She sang an experimental bar or two, as she dawdled on the stairs.

"I never thought I'd be the one to say
A day is something more than just a day . . ."

"Lynne!" her mother called warningly.

"Coming, Mom," Lynne called back, bounding down the last few stairs. "Sorry," she added hastily as she slipped into her chair at the table. "I got ready as fast as I could."

Mrs. Henry's eyes were filled with concern as she regarded her daughter. "Honey," she began, obviously trying hard to say the right thing, "I want you to come to work with me this Saturday and let me have Rhoda do something with your hair. I know you don't like being fussed over, but, sweetheart, it really—"

Lynne felt her chin sticking out the way it always did when her mother started in on her. "I *like* my hair," she said fiercely. "And I don't want Rhoda putting that goop all over me the way she does on everybody."

Her mother's expression began to darken slightly. "You know, Lynne, you're making a statement to other people with the way you look. You're telling them you don't care about yourself. If you'd just take a little bit of time . . ."

Lynne felt tears welling up in her eyes. "I know I'm no beauty, Mom," she said roughly, pushing her cereal bowl away in disgust. "You don't have to keep harping on it all the time. I'm not dumb. I understand you loud and clear!"

Mrs. Henry hesitated a moment, then said softly, "It isn't just your hair or your clothes. Honey, I'm worried about you. Your grades haven't been as good as they could be, either. If I hadn't woken you up, you might have missed class this morning because you overslept—"

"I have study hall first period, anyway," Lynne interrupted. But she felt a twinge of guilt. Her mother was right. Her grades *weren't* that great. Mostly C's and B's, when she knew she could do much better if she really wanted to. But

Lynne liked staying in the background. Why should she make an effort when it was so much easier just to be average?

"I don't like the thought of your staying up night after night, working on those songs of yours," her mother went on, not looking at her. "If it's interfering with your sleep, keeping you from getting to school on time—"

Lynne's eyes blazed. "Those songs of mine," she said angrily, "don't interfere with anything."

Mrs. Henry bit her lip. Her pretty face was filled with love and worry. "Lynne," she said softly, "don't shut me out. Don't get angry with me. You put that wall of yours up, and there's no way I can touch you!"

Lynne felt her chin sticking out again. She couldn't help it. Her mother made her so mad sometimes!

"I can't drive you to school, I'm afraid," her mother added, looking anxiously at her wristwatch. "I'm already five minutes late. What are you going to do? You've missed the bus."

"I'm going to walk," Lynne said, grabbing her backpack and shoving her notebook inside.

She had planned on walking anyway, she reminded herself.

Once outside, she took a deep breath and began to calm down. It was a beautiful morning. Humming a few bars of her new song under her breath, she set off down the street, her backpack bouncing as she walked.

At first she thought she was seeing things. Then she realized it actually was him. Again. Her heart was pounding.

"Lynne!" Guy said, crossing the street to join her. "I didn't think you ever walked to school!"

"I overslept," she admitted, smiling shyly at him. All her anger and irritation vanished, and suddenly Lynne wanted only to please. "What about you? Don't you ever take the bus?"

"I like to walk," he told her, grinning. "The fresh air wakes me up—and I need it, especially since The Droids practice so late two or three times a week. I really need the extra time to get myself going in the morning. I'm a night person," he confided, looking right into her eyes as he spoke. "You know what I mean? I feel like I get my best work done really late at night, when everyone else is asleep."

"I know exactly what you mean," Lynne murmured, thinking about her song.

"Most people think I'm nuts," he told her, looking as if he really cared what her response was. "My mother, for instance, would do anything if I'd just forget about music. She wants me to be a doctor like my older brother."

"You can't listen to her!" Lynne said warmly.

Then she blushed, afraid she had been too vehe-
ment, but Guy looked delighted.

"You really think I shouldn't? How do I know
I'm good enough, though," he worried. "That's
what really gets to me. If I don't make it in the
end, after giving up so much . . ."

Lynne remembered then what her father had
gone through. She wished she knew Guy well
enough to confide in him. She wanted to tell him
that nothing was worth the sacrifice of a dream.
But instead she just said again, emphatically,
"You've got to stick with it, Guy. Besides, you
are good. Really good."

"You honestly think so?" he asked, his face
lighting up.

"I honestly think so," she said. She meant it
with all her heart.

Lynne felt as if she were walking on air for the
next six or seven blocks. She couldn't believe
how easy it was to be with Guy. He was so forth-
right, so eager to talk about himself and his feelings. It was as if they'd known each other for
months, even years! Best of all, he didn't press
her or ask her questions. That was what had so
often interfered with Lynne's friendships. She
hated being put on the spot. But Guy didn't ask
her anything, yet he listened carefully to everything she had to say. Even better, he seemed to
like her.

"You're a wonderful listener," Guy said feelingly. "You know, I've never met a girl I could talk to like this."

"I love hearing about music," she said, staring at the ground. "I guess I've never really known anyone I could ask about what it's like to play in a real live band!" Her eyes shone behind her glasses. "I can't believe how lucky you are," she added shyly.

Guy looked as though he was about to answer when a sudden blast from a car horn made them both look up in surprise. It was Jessica Wakefield, waving wildly at them from the driver's seat of the little red Fiat Spider the twins shared. Elizabeth had a doctor's appointment that morning, and Jessica was alone.

"Guy!" she called brightly, tossing her blond hair back so it shimmered in the sunlight. "This must be my lucky day! I've been trying to find you for *days!*"

"You have?" Guy said, surprised.

Lynne felt as if her feet were glued to the pavement. She couldn't get over how gorgeous Jessica looked in that shiny red sports car. She looked like an actress in a movie—her tanned skin, her perfect hair, her sparkling bluish-green eyes. Lynne would have given anything in the whole world to be Jessica Wakefield just then. It wasn't just her beauty, either, Lynne thought, Jessica was so confident. It was perfectly natural for *Jessica* to say she'd been looking for someone like Guy. Lynne herself would rather die than admit that *she*'d been looking for a boy! But Jessica made it sound like the most natural thing in the world.

"Didn't Dana tell you?" Jessica demanded, eyes widening in disbelief. "The cheerleaders are throwing a big dance in the gym next Saturday night, and we're positively *dying* for The Droids to play. Let me give you a ride to school," she begged him impulsively. "We *have* to talk, Guy!"

Guy looked questioningly at Lynne. "But—"

"Go ahead," Lynne said in a low voice, her heart pounding. She didn't expect Jessica to include *her* in the invitation. Why bring along excess baggage?

Jessica didn't even seem to notice Lynne. "Come on," she sang out. "You have to help me out, Guy. I'm just *desperate*!"

"Would you mind, Lynne?" Guy asked uncomfortably, shifting his weight from one foot to the other. "Maybe we could talk again later, after school or something."

"I don't mind," Lynne said, her throat aching from the knot that had suddenly formed. "Go ahead, Guy. I'll see you around sometime."

Guy flashed her a dazzling smile. "You're a real sport, you know that?" he said. And the next minute he was bounding across the road, opening the door on the passenger's side of

Jessica's car and slipping in beside her. Jessica flipped her hair back, said something Lynne couldn't hear, and laughed, a silvery peal of laughter that made Lynne's heart drop down to knee level.

She's laughing at me, Lynne thought woodenly, watching the red sports car pull away.

Lynne took a deep breath, fighting tears. She couldn't believe what a fool she'd been to think it was going to be any different with Guy. OK, so he loved music as much as she did. That didn't mean he wasn't a normal, red-blooded boy who could easily be charmed by a beautiful girl. What was it he said he liked about Linda Ronstadt? She couldn't remember, but Lynne was sure the beauty of Ronstadt's face had struck him as much as the beauty of her *voice*. Thank heavens Lynne hadn't told him she played the guitar or wrote music. He probably would have laughed at her.

As she walked the last few blocks to school, Lynne felt numb. By the time she had made it to the front door, homeroom was about to begin. The halls were crowded with students, and she looked around her, a strange, blank expression on her face, like a terrified child on a diving board, staring down at the water.

Another long day was ahead of her. She plunged numbly into the crowded corridor, barely noticing the excited chatter around her.

People were talking about their classes, the upcoming Rock Around the Clock relay the cheerleaders were organizing, and the junior-class softball game scheduled for Friday afternoon at Secca Lake.

But no one talked to Lynne.

And why should they? she asked herself. This was a day like any other. So why in the world should she expect anybody to pay her the slightest bit of attention? She was alone, and it looked as if that was the way it was going to stay.

Four

"Elizabeth," Jessica wailed, bending over to tug on the brand-new lace anklets she was wearing. "We're never going to catch up with Ken and Winston and those guys if you keep reading and rereading that stuff! Do you want to *walk* to Secca Lake?"

Elizabeth laughed as she glanced at the last few lines of the copy she had typed that morning for the next "Eyes and Ears" column. "The Droids are still talking about a song contest," her column concluded. "Can we expect to find a brand-new songwriter in our midst any day now?"

"I'm ready," she told her twin, slamming her notebook shut. It was Friday afternoon, and the twins were supposed to meet a big group out in the parking lot of Sweet Valley High—Ken,

37

Winston, Bill Chase, DeeDee Gordon, Enid, Roger Patman, Olivia Davidson—before dividing up into cars and driving out to Secca Lake. That afternoon was the junior-class softball game, sponsored each year by Mr. Collins and Mr. Jaworski. Not everyone played, but everyone joined in on the fun, enjoying an afternoon of sunshine on the beautiful fields surrounding the sparkling lake. Elizabeth was looking forward to the afternoon as much as Jessica.

"Hey!" Enid called a few minutes later, hurrying across the parking lot to join the twins. "We've all been wondering what was holding you two up. We could hardly get started without our favorite first basewoman!"

Elizabeth linked her arm through Enid's. "I'm afraid my softball arm is a little rusty," she said ruefully. "It's worn out from frantically trying to rewrite the 'Eyes and Ears' column!"

"It took her forever," Jessica grumbled. "And the worst thing is, she only wrote one sentence on the most important piece of news!"

"So that's what's bugging you." Elizabeth laughed. "You mean the Rock Around the Clock relay, I take it?"

"What else?" Jessica demanded, aggrieved. "The biggest event of the *year*," she complained to Enid, "and our ace reporter here practically ignores it."

"I'm all for the relay, Jess," Elizabeth said

dryly, "but frankly, eight girls and one rocking chair is *not* my idea of the biggest event of the year. Besides," she said and giggled, "you guys have advertised this thing well enough without my help. You must have thirty signs up in the main hall alone!"

Jessica pouted. "Eight girls and one rocking chair," she repeated moodily. "Is that the way you see it?" Her aqua eyes darkened as she regarded her twin. "For your information, we have permission from the office to have a dance in the gym from eight till eleven on Saturday, and The Droids have agreed to play. *And* we've lined up teachers who will take turns staying up and monitoring us. It's turning into the biggest event of the whole semester!"

Enid and Elizabeth exchanged glances.

"Jess, I think the relay's a great idea," Elizabeth said consolingly. "Honestly. You know I backed it from the start! And now that you've gotten The Droids to play, it's guaranteed to be a great success! I just wasn't sure it was really the right kind of news to *highlight* in the column, that's all."

Jessica looked somewhat mollified. "It's really going to be a great time," she said, brightening in anticipation. "We're each going to rock for an hour at a time. There are eight of us, so that means we'll each have to take three turns. The only bad part is going to be in the middle of the night, but at least we'll be able to keep each other company."

Enid laughed. "You're going to need it at three in the morning," she joked.

By now the three had joined the group gathered at the end of the parking lot. "What a day for a softball game," Ken Matthews was saying, glancing up appreciatively at the cloudless sky.

"Let's get going!" Jessica exclaimed. "I want to get to Secca Lake so I can start getting pledges for next Saturday night." She glanced meaningfully around the circle. "I know *you* guys are all going to pledge me a dollar an hour, right?"

"You're off your rocker," Winston joked, ignoring the groans around him.

"Don't you know puns are the lowest form of humor?" Enid teased Winston, her green eyes sparkling.

"Give him time," Jessica retorted. "I guarantee he'll come up with something lower!"

Elizabeth barely noticed the banter around her as her friends began to argue over which cars to take. Her eye was on a scene taking place several yards away, next to the new silver van that belonged to Max Dellon, the lead guitar player for The Droids. Guy Chesney was talking animatedly to Lynne Henry, his hands moving expressively as he spoke. Lynne appeared to be listening attentively.

What a difference, Elizabeth thought. She had

barely recognized Lynne at first—that was how powerful a change a smile could make!

Lynne looked as if she were really having fun, Elizabeth realized. And once again she wondered what kind of person had been hiding behind the sullen expression the girl usually wore.

With a smile on her face and a sparkle in her eye, Lynne Henry was actually almost pretty!

"Don't you feel like playing?" Lynne asked uncertainly, standing in the shade of an enormous oak tree near the baseball diamond, nervously twisting a bit of leaf she'd scooped up from the grass.

Guy shook his head. "I'm not that big on sports," he confided. "Why don't we just sit down for a while and watch?"

"OK," Lynne said, feeling a little dazed. She still couldn't believe she had actually come to Secca Lake with Guy. When he had asked her if she wanted a ride, she couldn't believe her ears. Guy didn't have a car, having sold his station wagon a few months earlier, but he said there was plenty of room in Max's van and Max wouldn't mind. And sure enough, he hadn't. The van had been so crowded that one extra person hadn't made much difference.

The funny thing was that Lynne hadn't been the slightest bit nervous during the ride out to the park grounds. The atmosphere in the van had been so relaxed and lighthearted that she felt perfectly at ease. No one had talked to her after saying a casual hello, but that was fine with her. She just wanted to observe, to listen to every word they said. The Droids had always been her biggest heroes. Lynne knew every song they played, and sometimes when she played the guitar, she imagined she was Dana Larson, the sleek, trendy blond who was their lead singer.

Now, though, the Droids had scattered, and she was alone with Guy. Her old clumsiness had come back, and she felt tongue-tied and miserable.

But Guy didn't seem to be aware of her discomfort. Plopping down on the soft grass, he sighed with contentment, observing the scene before him. "What a perfect day," he mused.

"I usually hate things like this," Lynne said, more to herself than to Guy. Her face flushed. *What an idiot*, she reprimanded herself sharply. *That's hardly a nice thing to tell someone like Guy!*

His brown eyes widened. "Why?" he asked. But the way he said it, he didn't sound like her mother. He sounded concerned, as if he really wanted to know why she felt the way she did.

"I don't know." Lynne shrugged. "I've always been kind of a loner. My father died when I was really little, and I've had to fend for myself for so long that I guess I've gotten almost *too* self-reliant. I'm not really a people-person," she concluded.

Guy picked a blade of grass, then regarded her thoughtfully. "That's interesting," he said. "It sounds kind of familiar. Sometimes I feel that I'm not very good with crowds, either. I tell myself it's partly because of my music, because I need time alone to work. Maybe you're the same way. Maybe you have an artistic temperament, too."

Lynne looked away, embarrassed. It was as if Guy could see right inside her, straight through to her innermost thoughts. "No," she said simply, "I don't think so. I think I'm just shy."

Suddenly there were so many things she wanted to tell Guy. She wanted to tell him all about her guitar, about the lessons she had started giving at the Music Center. But she couldn't. She was afraid he would laugh at her and think she was a fool to expect to make it in a competitive world like the music industry.

Instead she sat back and listened to Guy. She was amazed at how easy it seemed to be for him to share things. He talked so naturally about his childhood, his devotion to music, his ambitions. "I'm going to try to get accepted to a music conservatory when I graduate from high school," he was saying. "I couldn't stand going to a regular college. Maybe Juilliard," he added. Otherwise, he was going to try to get into another band, try to fight his way to the top somehow.

Lynne closed her eyes briefly. She had a sudden vision of Guy playing keyboard for a chart-topping band. She could see him perfectly, playing his heart out, and next to him, in a glittery white dress, the singer who had made the group's success possible: Lynne Henry. Her hair redone, her skin glowing, her voice so vibrant and beautiful that the crowds were swooning. Afterward everyone would try to fight for her autograph, but Guy would pick her up in his arms and run through the throngs to the nearby limousine. "You were wonderful," he'd say. "Just like always, Lynne." And then, the most magical moment of all: he would lean closer and closer, his lips touching hers, her arms tightening around his neck as they kissed passionately—

"Guy!" Dana Larson called, interrupting Lynne's reverie. "Come on. We've been looking everywhere for you. We want to announce our new song contest before the game gets under way."

Guy jumped to his feet. "Sorry," he said to Lynne. "I'll be back in a few minutes."

Lynne mumbled something, wishing she could, for once in her life, say something appropriate at a moment like this. She always felt like a prize moron about things that no one else would even blink at!

What song contest? she was wondering,

getting clumsily to her feet and following Guy and Dana across the sunny field. The junior class had gathered at the baseball diamond, and Mr. Collins was blowing a whistle and waving his arms for everyone to be quiet.

"Welcome to the annual junior-class softball game," he said, smiling at the roar of applause that greeted his words. He waited a minute for everyone to be quiet. "We've got a special announcement this afternoon from our very own rock group, The Droids, and I promised them they could have the floor—or, should I say, the *diamond*—before we choose teams and get this ball game under way."

A hush fell over the crowd.

Dana Larson took Mr. Collins's place on the pitcher's mound, and the rest of The Droids gathered around her. "We just wanted to let all of you know that we're officially starting our Star-Search Song Contest," Dana announced. "We're posting signs all over school and running an ad in *The Oracle*, but we thought we'd tell you guys firsthand this afternoon. Any student at Sweet Valley High is eligible to enter the contest. Songs *have* to be original and should be submitted by cassette to the *Oracle* office."

"By when?" DeeDee Gordon asked from the back of the crowd.

"We'll be accepting entries between now and next Friday at noon," Dana said, putting her

45

hands up when a few people booed. "I know, I know," she said. "That's only a week. But songwriters always have to work under pressure! We're looking for something really special," she added. "Something fresh and new with a lot of heart—not just the same rock song without any meaning." She paused and looked around at her attentive classmates. "The winner's song," she concluded dramatically, "will be performed at our next big gig."

This news was greeted with a burst of spontaneous applause. Lynne turned away, her heart hammering. She couldn't believe it—it was like a dream come true! Ignoring the chattering students around her, who were pushing forward to be chosen for teams, Lynne made her way back to the place where she and Guy had been sitting. A song contest, a chance to find out once and for all if she had any real talent! And she would really give the contest her best effort. Especially now that she knew Guy would help judge the tapes.

And the prize! Lynne tried to imagine one of her songs actually being performed by The Droids. It would be a dream come true.

Are you crazy? she thought suddenly, furious with herself for being such a jerk. She couldn't enter the song contest. There was no way she could let anyone hear a cassette of her singing. She'd rather die.

She was on the outside, and that was all there was to it. On the outside looking in.

The outside looking in. . . . That sounded like a song title! she thought. Her brow knotted with concentration, Lynne tried to imagine those words set to music. She felt the electric current running through her that meant she was on to something—something good.

I don't care, she thought suddenly, her eyes flashing with determination. She *was* going to enter that contest. She was going to write the best song she possibly could, and she wasn't going to worry about what would happen if anyone heard her sing on tape, either. Because she wasn't going to put her name on the cassette she submitted.

People wrote anonymous poems and anonymous letters to the editor and anonymous graffiti—so why couldn't she write an "anonymous" song?

"Anonymous," she said aloud, half bitterly and half seriously.

It was the mask that was going to allow Lynne Henry to show everyone what she was really about. And it was going to be a really special song, too. It was going to be written for all the "nobodies" out there: for anyone who knew what it felt like to be anonymous when everyone else had a name—for anyone who had ever known what it was like to be on the outside, looking in.

Five

"Lynne," Mrs. Henry said, poking her head inside the door to Lynne's room, "I was wondering if we could have a talk."

Lynne was sitting on her bed, her guitar in her arms. "Could it wait, Mom? I'm right in the middle of—"

"Not really," her mother interrupted, opening the door wider. "Sweetie, I thought you were going to do your homework after dinner from now on! Didn't we decide that would be the best way to get your grades up?"

Lynne bit her lip. "We" hadn't decided anything of the sort, she thought. Her mother was the one who had done all the deciding, as usual. "I'm writing a song," Lynne said quietly. "And I don't have any homework today, Mom. We had a softball game out at Secca Lake, so we missed all our afternoon classes."

Mrs. Henry's face softened. "Secca Lake," she said dreamily. "That's such a beautiful place. Did you—" She hesitated, looking as if she were trying to think of the right way to word what she wanted to ask. "Did you have a good time?" she asked finally.

"It was OK," Lynne said noncommittally, wishing her mother would go back downstairs and leave her alone.

But Mrs. Henry didn't seem to be going anywhere. "Lynne, I know you don't like it when I pry," she began.

Lynne's face tightened up automatically. "Not really," she mumbled.

"But I was wondering if you're finding it any easier at school now." Mrs. Henry looked embarrassed and disappointed at the same time. Lynne pushed her glasses up on her nose, the way she always did when she was nervous or upset. "School's OK," she said, knowing she sounded about as thrilled as if she'd been asked if she would like to go have a few cavities filled.

"Oh, Lynne," her mother said suddenly, tears filling her beautiful eyes. "I feel so bad when you won't even talk to me! Don't you think I know how it feels to be lonely?"

Lynne stared at her mother. "I don't know what you're talking about," she said dully. Her throat ached. She didn't know why she acted like such a brat around her mother. She loved her with all her heart. Her mother was all she had, and she would die if anything ever happened to her. Yet she couldn't bring herself to do anything her mother asked. "I'm sorry," she said woodenly, still clutching her guitar. "I don't know what's the matter with me, Mom. I guess I'm just a big zero in every department!"

Mrs. Henry went over and put her arms around Lynne, who stiffened, hating herself. "Listen, sweetie," her mother said, tears running down her cheeks. "I don't think you're a zero! I just think you're unhappy. And I want to help you somehow. If only you wouldn't shut me out—"

"I'm not unhappy," Lynne said flatly. *I'm miserable*, she thought. But somehow she couldn't admit it to her mother. It seemed like the ultimate defeat.

"Well," her mother said at last, her face tearstained and confused, "I guess I should just leave you alone if you're working on a song, hmm?"

Lynne felt like crying. She didn't want her mother to go. She wanted to put her arms around her and weep her heart out on her shoulder. She wanted to tell her all about Guy and how confused she had been feeling since she met him. But she couldn't.

"I guess you should," she said dully, watching with a face of stone while her mother crossed the room and shut the door behind her.

The minute the door closed, Lynne strummed an experimental D-minor chord on her guitar. The melancholy chord suited her mood perfectly. Closing her eyes, she tried to feel her way back toward the magical tingling that had begun earlier that day when the phrase "outside, looking in" had come into her mind. She tried to clear her mind, keeping herself as still as possible. Strumming another chord, she half-whispered, half-sang the phrase, "Day after day, I'm feeling kind of empty." She frowned, shook her head, and reached for her notebook and pencil. "Day after day I'm feeling kind of lonely," she wrote. A smile crossed her face. That was better. "Day after day, it's him and him only." Tears filled her eyes. She had never felt this way writing a song before. This was her life she was writing about— her loneliness, her pain, her awkwardness. The song came as if from out of nowhere. She wasn't even aware of the minutes flying past, and she couldn't believe her eyes when she looked up at last, the finished lyrics scrawled hastily on her note pad. It was ten o'clock already. She had been working for almost two hours.

But she couldn't wait to record the song. She felt as if she had to do it *now*, before she lost heart and forgot the whole thing. Her fingers trembling, she set her tape recorder up, inserting a blank cassette and placing the microphone carefully on her bed so it wouldn't jiggle. At last everything was ready. She pushed the record button and sang her song. She couldn't believe how confident she felt. Her voice was rich and full, without a single quaver in it, and tears stung her eyes from the depth of emotion she was feeling. There was no doubt about it: everything she had was in this song. If The Droids didn't like it, it wasn't because she hadn't tried.

"There!" she said at last. She labeled the tape " 'On the Outside, Looking In' (Anonymous)" and dropped it in an envelope. "There," she said again, but she didn't feel triumphant any more.

She knew she had given the song everything she had. She just wished she could somehow let Guy know she had written it for him.

But it was better this way, she tried to reassure herself. Being anonymous meant no glory, no recognition. But it also meant no risk of pain. And she wasn't going to risk being hurt, not for anything in the world.

Not even for Guy Chesney.

It was Monday afternoon, and Elizabeth and Enid, were in the Wakefield's living room, listening to records Enid had brought over. Their conversation drifted languidly from one topic to another. "Billie Holiday is really something,"

Enid said admiringly. "I think this is my favorite album."

Elizabeth nodded in agreement. She adored the blues singer as much as Enid did. She decided at that moment to go record shopping later that week and to buy a Billie Holiday album for herself.

"Speaking of music, what do you think about the contest The Droids are running?" Elizabeth asked.

Enid's green eyes sparkled. "I think it's so exciting," she said and sighed. "A real star search, right in Sweet Valley High! Do you think they'll get a lot of entries?"

"I should hope so, considering how well they're advertising," Elizabeth replied. "I don't know, though," she reconsidered. "I'm not sure how many songwriters are hiding out there. Maybe not that many."

"Well, I hope they find the perfect song," Enid said vehemently. "The Droids are so good. If they could find a terrific song, I bet they'd make it in no time."

"Who'd make it in no time?" Jessica demanded, appearing in the doorway with her usual eager and inquisitive expression on her face.

Elizabeth groaned. "The walls have ears," she complained.

"We're talking about The Droids," Enid told

Jessica. "We were just saying that they could use a really great song."

"I hope they find one by Saturday night," Jessica said. "We're going to need something wonderful to listen to. Otherwise, all those hours in the rocking chair might start to get a little dull."

Enid giggled. "Your bottom's going to be sore!"

"It'll be worth it," Jessica said stoically. "You should see the outfits we decided on yesterday. They're so cute—little white skirts and the sweetest short-sleeved tops. We're just a few pledges short of having the best-looking uniforms in the whole state!"

"Did you get a lot of pledges at lunch today?" Enid asked. "I saw you running around like crazy in the cafeteria."

"I did pretty well," Jessica said modestly. "Do either of you want to guess how much money I'll raise each hour I rock?"

"Break it to us, Jess." Elizabeth said. "How much?"

"Twenty-five dollars," Jessica said proudly. "That makes seventy-five dollars if I rock for three hours. That's pretty good for one night's fund-raising, don't you think?"

"Excellent," Enid said.

"I have to go," Jessica announced. "The cheerleaders are meeting over at Helen Bradley's house. She's got a rocking chair, and we have to practice."

Elizabeth and Enid fought hard to keep their faces straight. "I hope it goes well," Elizabeth said, losing her composure.

"Cut it out," Jessica said, pouting. "You guys are going to be sorry Saturday night that you made fun of me. You're going to wish *you* could be in on the relay, too."

"Maybe you could start a new fad," Elizabeth said, wiping tears of laughter from her eyes. "Instead of collecting rocks, you could get people collecting rockers!"

"I'm leaving," Jessica said, storming out of the room.

Enid and Elizabeth locked gazes. That was all it took. The next minute they were laughing so hard they thought they'd never be able to stop.

"What's wrong?" Jessica demanded, looking around in dismay at the deadpan faces that greeted her in the Bradleys' comfortable living room.

"Hellen just made us all feel rotten, that's all," Annie Whitman said, reaching over to take a brownie from the tray on the coffee table. "Tell her the awful news, Helen."

Helen blinked miserably. "I'm the one who should be sad, not you guys," she said, refusing to meet Jessica's inquisitive gaze. "My dad just told us that he and my mom went ahead and bought the house of their dreams," she admitted after a long, glum silence "But it's in Los Angeles! I still can't believe it," she moaned, staring around at the others with a stricken look on her face. "I can't believe we have to move away from Sweet Valley!"

"When are you supposed to move?" Jessica demanded.

"It could be practically any time." Helen sighed. "My dad said he's putting our house on the market right away. It could be next week, or the week after—"

Jessica went pale. "But what about the squad?" she cried. "Helen, we're counting on you! You can't drop out of cheerleading after everything we've been through together!"

"Jessica," Cara pointed out, "what's she supposed to do, commute from Los Angeles? Be reasonable!"

Jessica grimaced. Be reasonable, indeed. She and Robin Wilson were co-captains of the team, but *she* was the one who had ended up doing most of the work the last time they had had auditions. Granted, that was at her own insistence. But she couldn't stand the thought of going through that again. They finally had a squad that worked well together!

Helen left the room for a minute, and Cara turned to Jessica, keeping her voice low. "It's hardly going to make Helen feel any better, hearing you gripe about her leaving the cheerleaders."

"That's easy for *you* to say," Jessica retorted. She was thinking that *she* was the one who had to suffer most when they had auditioned Annie Whitman, but she didn't dare mention it, not with Annie right in the room. The poor girl had tried to commit suicide when she hadn't made the squad. Everyone had gone almost crazy with fear and worry. Finally they expanded the squad and let her on. The last thing Jessica wanted was to go through something like that again.

"Lighten up," Cara whispered to Jessica. "The poor girl's really low about moving as it is."

"OK, OK," Jessica conceded. But her spirits were considerably dampened. The rest of the evening dragged, and Jessica could barely wait to get home to tell her sister the grim news about Helen.

She and Cara were the last to leave. After they had said goodbye to Helen, Cara put her hand on Jessica's arm, her face bright with excitement. "I couldn't tell you the news before," she confided, her pretty eyes sparkling, "because it seemed too cruel after Helen dropped her bombshell. Did Lila ever tell you about her fabulous, adorable cousin Christopher?"

Jessica stopped short. "The really cute one who lives in New England somewhere?"

"That's right." Cara was positively brimming with excitement. "He's seventeen, and he lives in Kennebunkport, Maine. The incredible news is that he's coming out to the West Coast to visit Lila!"

"When?" Jessica demanded, her eyes widening. This *was* good news!

"Not for a few weeks. That's why I didn't want to say anything in front of Helen," Cara replied. "I thought it would just add insult to injury, since she may have moved by the time he gets here. And, Jess, Lila says she's going to have the biggest, most fabulous party ever, to celebrate his arrival!"

Jessica laughed. Lila's parties were famous in Sweet Valley, and she had a hard time imagining how she could compete with her own past success. But she had a feeling Lila would find a way.

And somehow the news about Christopher made it easier for Jessica to put Helen Bradley's move out of her mind. Helen herself had said it could be weeks before they actually left Sweet Valley. *Why worry about it now?* she asked herself. She had too much to look forward to in the next few days to worry about cheerleading auditions.

And she was bound and determined to make sure Saturday's Rock Around the Clock was as fun an event as she had promised all her classmates!

Six

It was Wednesday morning. Lynne swallowed nervously. *This is it*, she told herself, checking both sides of the hallway to make sure no one was coming. It was first period, her study hall, and she wanted to drop her cassette off in the box in the *Oracle* office when no one else would see her. This seemed like the best possible time, when everyone else was in class.

For the dozenth time, Lynne wondered if she was doing the right thing. Why submit the song at all? Wasn't she risking being found out? *No way*, she assured herself, checking her bag to make sure the envelope was still there. No one could possibly figure out who the anonymous singer was. Taking a deep breath, she hurried across the hall and put her hand on the doorknob to open the door to the office. To her shock and dismay, the door was pulled open, and Elizabeth Wakefield hurried out, almost knocking Lynne off her feet.

"Lynne!" Elizabeth said, obviously startled, too. "I'm so sorry. Are you OK?"

"Y-y-y-yes," Lynne stammered, turning scarlet. "It was my fault, anyway."

Elizabeth's face relaxed into a smile. "It's the *door*'s fault," she said and giggled. "We have no-fault accidents around this office all the time!"

Lynne could feel her heart hammering. She was cursing herself out for not having considered that someone might be *inside* the office. Any second now Elizabeth was going to ask her what she was doing there, and Lynne would be found out. She felt terrible, and she was sure her secret was written all over her face.

"Can I help you with something?" Elizabeth asked. "Did you want to come inside?"

Lynne blinked, feeling ridiculous. "Uh—no, Liz. I actually had the wrong room, if you can believe that." She laughed, a false, absurd-sounding laugh that made her cringe. Elizabeth looked at her strangely but didn't say anything.

"Well, I'd better run," Elizabeth said, still looking closely at Lynne. "You're sure you don't need anything?"

"Sure," Lynne said with exaggerated cheer.

"OK." Elizabeth closed the door behind her,

gave Lynne a parting smile, and hurried down the hall.

That was close, Lynne thought. She waited until Elizabeth had turned the corner before opening the door. Then she scuttled into the office, made sure no one else was around, and dropped her envelope into the box marked Droids' Songwriting Contest Submissions. Wiping her forehead with the back of her sleeve, Lynne darted back into the hall, pulling the door closed and breathing an enormous sigh of relief.

She'd done it. No one could possibly figure out who the anonymous singer was. There was no way that Elizabeth could make the connection, either. There were already several cassettes in the box, and no one would suspect the yellow envelope was any different from the other submissions.

Lynne felt an enormous sense of relief. She had managed to submit her song without being discovered. She had put everything she had into that song, stripping herself bare, revealing her deepest feelings for the very first time. If anyone thought she was the one singing those words, it would be the end of her.

But the way she had handled it, she was sure no one would ever find out about her song.

A small crowd had gathered out on the rolling green lawn under the big oak trees in front of

Sweet Valley High. It was one o'clock on Friday afternoon, and the lunch hour was drawing to a close. The Droids were at the center of the group, reading aloud the names of the submissions they had received and popping the cassettes into a battery-operated cassette player. Elizabeth and Jessica were listening avidly with the rest of the group, waiting for the perfect song, the special hit that would become a signature title for The Droids. The four songs they had heard so far all sounded very much the same. They were nice, but nothing special.

"I don't know," Elizabeth said, looking disturbed. "It doesn't seem as if they're going to find what they're looking for after all."

"Hey, what's this?" Guy said, taking a tape out of a yellow envelope and turning it over in his hands. "It's marked Anonymous," he said, looking at it speculatively. " 'Outside, Looking In,' by *Anonymous*!"

"What kind of title is that?" Ken Matthews asked. " 'Outside, Looking In.' It sounds kind of strange."

"Let's give it a try," Guy said, popping the tape into the cassette player. A hush fell over the group as he pushed the play button. For a moment the only sound was the whirring of the tape player. Then there was an introductory chord or two from a guitar, followed by one of

64

the richest, throatiest, most gorgeous voices they had ever heard.

"Jeez," Ken said, sitting up straighter. "Whoever she is, she can really sing!"

"Ssssh!" Guy said, his expression transfixed. He turned the volume up. "Listen to the words!"

Elizabeth felt her spine prickling as the haunting melody poured out of the tape player. She couldn't believe anyone her own age could have written a song with so much maturity, such deep and poignant feeling.

"Wait!" Guy cried. "We have to rewind this and play it from the beginning. I had no idea anyone around here could write like this!"

This time the audience was ready from the beginning for the magic they were about to hear. The chords struck up again, and the haunting voice sang the poignant lyric from the first word:

Day after day I'm feeling kind of lonely,
Day after day it's him and him only.
Something in his eyes
Made my hopes start to rise.

But he's part of a world that doesn't include me.
Nothing he says could ever delude me.
I'll never win.
This is how it's always been.
I'm on the outside . . . looking in.

Night after night I'm saying a prayer
Night after night . . . that somebody will
care!
Somebody to hear me,
Someone to stay near me . . .

But nothing's going to change. Dreams can't
deceive me.
I'm all alone. You've got to believe me.
I just can't win.
This is how it's always been . . .
I'm on the outside—on the outside . . .
Lookin' in.

A hush fell over the group when the last note had faded. Guy, his eyes bright with excitement, grabbed Dana's arm. "That's it," he said, his voice choked with emotion. "That's the song we've been looking for!"

Everyone began to buzz with excitement. "It's such a beautiful song," Elizabeth said.

"Who do you suppose it could be?" Enid asked.

Guy jumped to his feet, his cheeks blazing. "OK," he said, obviously trying to control his excitement. "We've got a mission, you guys. We've got to find out who this anonymous songwriter is. Can I count on everyone to help me?"

"Don't you think that's going to be a little

hard?" Ken demanded. "Whoever this person is obviously doesn't want to be discovered. Why else wouldn't she submit the song under her name?"

"We've got to find her," Guy repeated stubbornly, rewinding the tape to play it again. His eyes were filled with a strange expression—something between awe and desperation. "Don't you understand? I've just *got* to find the girl who wrote this song!"

"Lynne," Mr. Collins said, standing up behind his desk and brushing his strawberry-blond hair back from his forehead, "would you mind staying behind for a few minutes? I want to talk to you about your paper on Emily Dickinson."

"Sure," Lynne mumbled. She wasn't in any hurry to eat her sandwich, anyway. The high point of the week, turning her song in at *The Oracle*, was over. Now she just wanted the hours to fly by. Soon she'd have the whole weekend to herself, to work on her music. And on Saturday she was teaching guitar at the Music Center.

Mr. Collins was frowning at her paper. Her throat felt dry. What had she done wrong? She had worked hard on the paper, harder than she usually did.

"Lynne, there are some very strong things in this essay," Mr. Collins said, looking directly at her. "You have original insights into Emily Dickinson's poetry, and you write very well."

"Thank you," Lynne said, feeling embarrassed. She had hardly expected him to *praise* her!

"In fact," Mr. Collins said, "I get the feeling you've got a lot of natural talent when it comes to writing. Have you written any poetry yourself?"

Lynne felt her cheeks redden. "N-no," she stammered. She wasn't exactly lying. Songs weren't poems, were they?

Mr. Collins looked at her, not saying anything for a minute. "If you ever *do* write something, I hope you feel that you can bring it to me. I'd be delighted to read it."

Lynne felt terrible. Mr. Collins was so nice, not jumping all over her for being so quiet in class or anything. She wished she had the courage to tell him about her songwriting. But she couldn't bring herself to say anything.

"Thanks," she mumbled, taking the paper from him. "I'm glad you think it's OK."

Mr. Collins laughed. "It's more than 'OK,' " he told her. His voice suddenly turned serious. "Lynne, one of these days you're going to realize that *you're* more than 'OK,' too. And you know something? I really hope I'm around to see the look on your face when you figure that out."

Lynne's eyes filled with tears. What did he mean, "more than OK"?

She found that hard to believe. And if Mr. Collins thought something miraculous was going to happen to make her change her mind about herself, he had another think coming.

Lynne Henry was still convinced she was the biggest nobody of all time.

Seven

Lynne was standing in front of her locker in the main hall, looking uneasily at the pile of books and papers she had been meaning to straighten up for ages. Her last-period class had finally ended, and the weekend was here. Why wasn't she as glad as she'd expected to be?

Mr. Collins's words kept resounding in her head. If only he were right—if only there really *were* something that could prove once and for all that she really mattered. Staring into her messy locker, Lynne found herself wondering if she shouldn't take her mother up on her offer for a day at the Silver Door. Maybe she should risk it—and try wearing her contact lenses and doing something with her hair.

Impulsively, Lynne slammed her locker shut and darted across the hall to the girls' bathroom.

71

Setting her backpack on the floor, she walked across the tiled room to the sink and looked apprehensively at herself in the mirror. *Good Lord*, she thought. She looked even worse than she had feared. Her hair was unusually frizzy that day, standing away from her head in a tangled halo. Her glasses were smudged, and in the fluorescent light of the bathroom, her skin looked even more sallow then usual. And her outfit! Lynne couldn't even remember getting dressed that morning, but whatever could have inspired her to wear the same grubby pair of blue jeans and her old navy T-shirt?

This is it, Lynne told herself, glaring at her reflection. *This is really it*. Suddenly she was fed up with herself for being such a slob. True, she might not have been blessed at birth in the beauty department, but that didn't mean she had to aggravate the situation by taking such bad care of herself.

Full of resolve, Lynne dashed out of the bathroom into the main corridor and smack into *him*. Her face turned bright red. "Guy . . ." she mumbled, stepping back clumsily and almost falling down.

Guy laughed, his arm shooting out to steady her. "Where are you racing off to?" he demanded.

Lynne swallowed hard. His hand was warm on her arm. "Actually, I'm just going home," she admitted. *Go on, ask him if* he's *walking home,* she instructed herself. But she just stood there, tongue-tied and awkward, wishing the floor would open up and she could disappear forever.

"Well, if you wait a minute, I'll join you," Guy said cheerfully. "I just have to pick up the cassettes."

"I'll wait here," Lynne said nervously. Somehow she had managed to put the songwriting contest out of her mind for the last few hours. But at Guy's reminder her heart began to pound. Maybe he had already listened to "Outside, Looking In." Maybe The Droids had *all* listened to it—and had decided to eliminate it! She was sure now that she had made a huge mistake believing her own work could stand up to the serious scrutiny of The Droids. Who did she think she was trying to fool?

"How's the song contest going?" she asked, dry-mouthed when Guy returned.

Guy's eyes lit up. "You won't believe it," he told her, opening the door for her and stepping after her into the warm, sweet-smelling afternoon. "We listened to the tapes at lunchtime, and the group is coming over tonight to listen to them again. But I think we've found exactly what we're looking for. This girl has written the most spectacular song. And she can sing, too! It's the sort of song that gives you the chills. You know what I mean?"

Lynne stared at him, crestfallen. He had already found his dream singer, and he hadn't even played her own tape yet! Her mouth tasted awful. She had a sudden image of Guy putting his arm around the winning songwriter, some curvacious girl with a gorgeous face. It wasn't fair, she thought bitterly.

"I really want you to hear this girl," Guy was going on, making her feel worse and worse. "I get the impression you really know a lot about female vocalists, Lynne. Tell me what you think," he added enthusiastically, taking his Walkman and a cassette out of his backpack. He popped the cassette into the player and handed Lynne the headphones.

Lynne's eyes widened with disbelief as her own voice sang out at her from the tiny foam headphones. Guy *had* listened to her cassette, and he liked it! What was it he had said? "The sort of song that gives you the chills . . ." Fighting to compose herself, Lynne listened to the entire song before taking the headphones off and passing Guy the Walkman.

"I don't know," she said cautiously, staring down at the pavement. "You really think she's that good?"

Guy shook his head impatiently. "She's awesome! I want to play it over and over again. I just can't get it out of my mind."

Lynne's face felt hot. "What about the lyrics?"

she asked him. "Do you think they're original enough?"

"Original?" Guy stared at her. "They're gorgeous. If only I could find this girl and tell her what I think of her . . ."

Lynne's pulse quickened. "What do you mean?" she asked carefully. "It should be easy enough to find her."

Guy shook his head ruefully. "That's the terrible thing," he moaned. "She didn't put her name on the tape! She entered it anonymously, believe it or not. It figures. The only truly spectacular entry we get, and we've got no way of finding the person who turned it in."

Lynne felt a wave of relief pass over her. She was safe then. The Droids didn't have the faintest idea who had written the song. "Maybe she'll come forward once you've announced the winner," Lynne said casually, thinking at the same time, *Not as long as I can help it, she won't!*

Guy frowned. "I hope so," he told her. "This girl is really special, Lynne. I mean, she really has talent! She's got the sort of voice that could go all the way to the top if she had the right kind of band to work with. Don't you see," he said, his voice heavy with agitation, "we've just *got* to find her!"

"I wonder what she's like," Lynne said, averting her eyes.

Guy was quiet for a minute. "I don't know,"

he said softly, his brown eyes shining. "But I have a feeling she's really intense—really terrific. I can just tell by listening to her that she's not like anybody else around here. Gosh," he concluded breathlessly, "can you just imagine what it would be like to actually play backups for her? It would be like a dream come true. Like playing for Linda Ronstadt," he added, smiling at her.

Lynne felt her mouth go dry. Guy probably thought this girl looked like Linda Ronstadt too.

Someone really special, he had said. Lynne didn't have to think too hard to imagine what *that* meant. Someone curvy, lithe, beautiful, someone who would look as good onstage as she sounded.

How right she'd been to keep her song anonymous! Lynne couldn't bear disappointing Guy, dashing his dream to bits. Let him keep thinking this anonymous songwriter was the girl he had been waiting for all his life.

Lynne knew better, and she was bound and determined no one else would learn the truth, however hard it became to keep her identity a secret.

"OK, Elizabeth Wakefield," Jessica cried, jumping into the passenger seat of the Fiat Spider beside her twin. It was Friday and the twins were about to drive home from school. "Are you going to tell me who this anonymous songwriter is, or do I have to force the truth out of you?"

Elizabeth laughed. "You flatter me," she said dryly. "Is that supposed to mean that I have ESP or something?"

Jessica frowned. "I'm serious, Liz. Cara and I have already decided that the Rock Around the Clock relay is the perfect place to unveil the mystery woman. It'll be a perfect attraction. But we can't unveil her till we find out who she is."

"That makes sense," Elizabeth said and giggled. "Your logic astounds me, Jess."

Jessica pouted. "I'm not kidding," she said. "Aren't you even going to tell your beloved sister? The person who's closer to you than anyone else in the whole wide world?"

Elizabeth laughed. "Would you really be surprised if I said I had no idea who this mysterious singer is?"

Jessica blinked. "I don't believe it. My sister, the ace reporter, the girl who always knows everything before anyone else. How could you possibly *not* know who this singer really is?"

"Because," Elizabeth said, starting the car up and pulling out of the parking place, "no one knows, Jess. That's the point, I guess. She really doesn't *want* anyone to know."

Jessica looked crushed. "Well, what kind of crummy joke is this? How in the world can we unveil her tomorrow night, then?"

Elizabeth laughed. "I guess you can't," she told her. "Don't you guys have enough going on tomorrow night as it is?"

"Well, I guess so. But it really seemed perfect. We had the whole thing worked out!"

"It *is* kind of strange," Elizabeth remarked. "Why do you suppose this girl doesn't want to take credit for her song? Especially since she's so obviously talented."

"You've got me," Jessica replied. "If *I* had written a song like that, you can bet I wouldn't keep it a secret!"

"It's hard to imagine you keeping anything a secret," Elizabeth said, smiling. Then her face became serious. "But it *is* strange, all the same. I wonder—"

"What?" Jessica demanded, knowing her sister well enough to suspect that the thoughtful expression on her face meant that she might be on to something.

Elizabeth frowned as she drove. "I don't know, Jess. But it does strike me as strange. And in a way it seems kind of sad, too. Because whoever wrote that song was pouring her heart out. It kind of makes you think—"

"Well, she can't expect anything else if she deosn't even let people know who she is," Jessica interrupted.

"Yes, but that may be part of the problem," Elizabeth mused. "That song is very personal, too. Whoever wrote it may not want to admit to having those feelings. Especially if she's a shy person or someone who isn't very secure about herself."

Jessica shrugged. "Maybe she'll turn herself in once she's won the contest. And from the way Dana and Guy were talking at lunch, I have a feeling she's got it all sewn up."

Elizabeth stopped at a red light and turned to Jessica, "Maybe we'll find more out tonight," she suggested. The twins were planning to go to the Beach Disco that night, a popular dance club right on the ocean. "Guy told me this afternoon that he's planning a serious search for this girl. And I have a feeling he may be starting his efforts tonight!"

Eight

By nine-thirty the Beach Disco was in full swing. The deejay was playing all the most popular songs, and the dance floor was crowded with students from Sweet Valley High. Jessica was dancing with Ken Matthews, her tight white jeans turning colors as the lights from above flashed on and off. Ken, the handsome blond captain of the football team, was fresh from a romantic disaster with Suzanne Hanlon, a spoiled, pretentious sophomore who had tried to "convert" Ken from a man of athletic prowess into a man of culture. Elizabeth was sitting this one out, already tired from her last dance with Winston Egbert. "I swear," she said jokingly to Enid, who was sitting across from her at a small table, "dancing with Winston is like running a marathon! That boy has the energy of five normal people."

Enid giggled. "Well, I could use a break myself," she told her friend, brushing her smooth brown hair away from her face. "Just between us," she added, dropping her voice, "I think Brent Stein is pretty terrific on the dance floor." Brent, a tall, serious senior with gray eyes and a satiric sense of humor, was Enid's latest secret crush.

"Hey," Elizabeth said suddenly, looking up. "Guy Chesney is coming over here. He seems kind of frantic."

"He's looking for the mysterious singer," Enid told her. "Something tells me he's about to ask you for help. Which tells *me*," she added, getting hastily to her feet, "that this is the perfect time to go see if I can't convince Brent Stein to dance the next song with me."

"You're abandoning me," Elizabeth accused.

"You're right," Enid said and giggled. "See you later."

The next minute Enid had slipped through the crowd, and sure enough, Guy had reached Elizabeth's table.

"Liz," he exclaimed when he was close enough to be heard over the music, "I've been looking for you everywhere!"

Elizabeth smiled. "Something tells me I'm not the only one you've been looking for," she said.

"But, Guy, I have no idea who this mysterious singer could be. Believe me, I'm as curious as everyone else is!"

"Liz," Guy said, upset, "could you come outside with me for just a couple of minutes? I can't even hear myself think in here."

"OK," Elizabeth said promptly. She liked Guy, and she wished there were something she could do to help him. At the very least, she was a sympathetic listener, and she was more than willing to duck outside with him for a breath of fresh air.

"Phew," Guy said, closing the door behind him and inhaling the mild night air. "God, there's nothing like the smell of the ocean," he added, giving Elizabeth a hand as they clambered up over the breakwater separating the disco from the smooth, sandy beach.

Elizabeth shivered involuntarily, looking at the oval of moonlight reflected on the wrinkling water before them. "It's gorgeous out here," she breathed.

Guy picked a shell up and skipped it across the water. "I love the water. When I was a kid, I used to sit on the beach for hours. I was convinced I could see China if I looked hard enough."

Elizabeth looked searchingly at Guy. "Only now you're not looking for China," she said softly, her turquoise eyes intent.

Guy's mouth tightened. "You're pretty perceptive, Liz. I guess that *is* why I wanted to come out here and look at the water. It always was magical to me. And tonight I guess I feel I need magic."

Elizabeth smiled at him. "I may be perceptive, but I'm not a magician," she told him. "I really wish I could help you find your mystery singer, but I haven't got a clue."

"Are you sure? Not the faintest idea who she could be?"

Elizabeth shook her head. Guy looked so disappointed she could have wept for him. "Honestly, Guy. I've got no idea." She thought for a minute. "Have you considered the fact that she may not *want* to be found out? I mean, the girl didn't enter that song anonymously just for kicks."

Guy's face darkened. "Liz, I have to find her! I keep playing that song over and over again, and it's like— I don't know. It's like it was written for me or something. That sounds weird, but I have the strangest sensation when I hear that girl's voice. It's like she's someone I've been searching for my whole life. I've just got to find her!"

Elizabeth listened wonderingly to the desperate sound in his voice. "I wish there was some way I could help you," she said softly.

"I just thought—you know, your working for *The Oracle* and all that—that maybe you'd be a good detective." He looked kind of embarrassed. "You know, everyone always says that you've got to be a sleuth to be a good reporter. And you're the best around! So I just hoped—"

Elizabeth shook her head and put her hand sympathetically on his arm. "I'd help if I could," she told him. "Honestly. But I haven't the faintest idea of where to begin. Even a good reporter needs a lead, and there doesn't seem to be anything to go on!"

"Well, thanks anyway," Guy told her, looking sadly out at the ocean. "I think I'll just stay out here for a while," he added when Elizabeth looked at him inquisitively. "Would you mind, Liz? I feel like I need to be alone, just to sort of think things over."

"Will you be all right?"

Guy nodded. "And thanks, Liz. I know if there were anything you could do, you'd do it. You're a good person."

Elizabeth sighed. She hated to leave him alone out there, so obviously disappointed. But she had told him the truth. She didn't have a clue to the identity of Guy's mystery singer.

"So what's going on with Guy?" Enid demanded, plopping down at the table again and taking a big sip of her soft drink. "Did you convince him that *I'm* really the one he's been searching for? The greatest musical talent in Sweet Valley High history?"

Elizabeth laughed affectionately. "You're too much, Enid. Actually," she said, dropping her voice, "I'm kind of worried about him. He really seems intense about this girl. I wonder if he's—"

"If he's what?"

Elizabeth frowned. "Well, it doesn't sound as if he's the head of a talent search anymore, if you know what I mean. He sounds like this girl is getting under his skin—like she's really beginning to matter, and not just as a songwriter."

Enid's green eyes widened. "You mean—"

Elizabeth stirred her root beer with a straw. "I think Guy Chesney is in love," she said finally, her eyes filled with concern. "The problem is, he doesn't even know this girl's *name*! And he hasn't got the faintest idea of how to find her, either."

"Gosh," Enid said, fascinated. "That's the most romantic thing I've ever heard in my whole life!" She looked across the room at Brent. "Maybe I could try it," she added, giggling at the thought. "Can you imagine me sending Brent a tape? 'Would you like to take a chance . . .' " she sang tunelessly. " 'Risk your feet and take this dance . . .' "

Elizabeth shook her head fondly. "You're nuts," she said. "Absolutely nuts. But seriously," she added, "I'm worried about Guy. I wonder how he's going to find her."

"I know," Enid said, her laughter fading. "It really is too sad for words. If only the girl would just confess and tell everyone who she is!"

"That would be wonderful," Elizabeth reflected. "But something tells me that that's not what's going to happen."

"I think you're right," Enid conceded. "So poor Guy is going to have to forget this girl or waste his time chasing after a phantom."

"I wonder," Elizabeth said musingly, "if the 'phantom' has any idea what a stir her song is causing right now."

Lynne was upstairs in her bedroom, frowning at the contents of her closet. Scattered around her on the floor were dozens of glamour and beauty magazines, each with a different suggestion: how to organize your closet, how to tone your thighs, how to highlight your hair, how to make your cheekbones look higher. It was mystifying, part of a world that Lynne had always refused to consider. She had to admit some of the articles were kind of fun. The idea of spending so much time on herself was—well, sort of decadent. And also sort of exciting!

It was Friday night, and her mother was out. Lynne was taking full advantage of her absence. She had spent the first part of the evening soaking in the bathtub, pouring first one mysterious lotion and then another under the steaming water. Oil of this, oil of that—she felt as if she were in a chemistry class!

Fresh from the bath, Lynne had wrapped herself in a huge, soft bath towel. And then, sitting down at the long gleaming counter under the fluorescent lights in the bathroom, she had looked long and hard at herself. She wanted to tweeze her eyebrows, but it was too hard with her glasses on. So, for the first time in months, Lynne put her contact lenses in. Plucking her eyebrows *hurt*! She kept sneezing, too. But the magazines had warned her that would happen. And she had to admit the final effect was kind of interesting. Her eyes looked even bigger than usual and farther apart.

Now, looking critically at the stacks of old jeans in her closet, she wondered if she could get away with what the magazines suggested for someone of her build. "Take full advantage of your height and slim figure," one article had insisted. "Wear bold colors, stripes, patterns— and don't slouch!"

"This stuff is awful," Lynne said aloud, looking at the grubby clothing she had been wearing for the past few years. It all looked like the stuff she had played football in when she was a scruffy little tomboy. She had to admit she'd been kind of blind to the way she was dressing. It definitely was time for a change.

At the very back of the closet were the clothes her mother had persistently bought for her each year at Christmas or on her birthday. Lynne had barely looked at them when she'd opened the packages, wishing she could have gotten records or sheet music instead. Now, for the first time, she looked. And some of the things weren't half bad. They were much flashier than she was used to, much brighter. At last she chose a cotton jumpsuit in a bright royal-blue print. It looked like something in that month's *Ingenue*, she thought. Again Lynne opened to the page in the magazine, determined to imitate the model as closely as possible. She layered the jumpsuit over a T-shirt, tied a sash around her waist, and even found a pair of her mother's earrings that didn't look half bad. "Hmmm," she said at last, considering the effect in her full-length mirror. She still wasn't gorgeous, but she had to admit she looked kind of interesting. For the first time Lynne realized that she didn't have to look like an oversized string bean. She could look tall and thin, the ideal according to all these magazines. And the brightly patterned jumpsuit actually made her look sophisticated and slender, instead of just skinny.

Anyway, she told herself, it was a start. Maybe when her mother came home Lynne could ask her for another chance at the Silver Door. Nothing drastic, but if she could do *something* with her hair and maybe get some tips about using makeup . . .

To her surprise, Lynne heard the sound of the front door opening downstairs. Her mother was home already, and she hadn't had time to clean the bathroom or get out of this weird costume or anything! Lynne's hands began to tremble as she fumbled with her mother's earrings. *She's going to laugh at me*, she was thinking hysterically. *She's going to think I look like a clown, that I'm a complete and utter joke . . .*

"Lynne?" Mrs. Henry was calling. "I decided to come home right after dinner. The line for the movie was just too long."

"I'll be right down, Mom!" Lynne yelled back, staring strickenly at herself in the mirror.

"Don't worry," her mother called back, halfway up the stairs. "I want to get out of these shoes anyway. They're killing my feet." Her voice got closer with each word and Lynne was frozen in place, feeling wretched. It was too late to do anything now. She was just going to have to face her mother.

"What're you doing, honey?" her mother asked. She knocked on her door and opened it a second later. "Can I come—" she began, but she never finished her question. "Lynne," she said in surprise. "You're wearing that jumpsuit I bought you."

"Don't laugh," Lynne choked out, her eyes filling with tears. "I just wanted to try—to try to look better—"

"Oh, sweetheart," her mother cried, crossing the room and throwing her arms around her daughter. "Lynne, you look wonderful! Really wonderful! And I would never, ever laugh at you," she added tenderly, stroking her daughter's hair as she rocked her in her arms. "You're all I've got in the whole world, sweetheart. Don't you know that?"

Lynne pulled away and stared at her mother. "Do you think I could come to the salon with you soon?" she asked. "I really want to try now, Mom. I'm sick of being such a mess."

"Oh, Lynne," her mother said, her voice choked up. "Of course you can come to the salon. But you're not a mess. You're—" Tears started down her face. "You're the most special girl in the whole world. You know that?"

Lynne stared at her mother dumbly, unable to say a word.

"That's much more important than coming to the Silver Door," her mother told her seriously. "What matters is feeling good about yourself— really good about yourself—and being able to see your strengths and talents as much as your weaknesses. Do you know what I'm saying?"

Lynne nodded, her throat aching. She knew exactly what her mother was saying. And for the first time in her life, she didn't push it aside or try to ignore her mother's advice. Because she knew now that she needed her mother's help. And she was ready and willing to try to change.

Nine

"Liz," Jessica said, hurrying into the Wakefields' pretty, Spanish-tiled kitchen, where her sister was finishing a bowl of cereal. "Want to see how many pledges I've gotten for tonight?" She thumped her clipboard down on the kitchen table with a triumphant flourish. "We're going to have the best uniforms ever! Don't you think I'll look great in a short white skirt?" She spun around, as if trying to imagine how the outfit would swirl, and Elizabeth burst out laughing.

"Kind of like counting your chickens before they've hatched, don't you think?" she asked, pushing aside the morning paper.

"I was wondering," Jessica said soberly, plopping down in a chair across from her twin, "if you feel like helping me take the rocking chair

93

over to the gym this morning and maybe helping with decorations. Are you doing anything?"

Elizabeth took a swallow of tea and shook her head. "Sorry. I want to run over to the Music Center and see if I can get that Billie Holiday album Enid has."

Jessica wrinkled her nose. "Ugh," she said. "Liz, don't you think Enid's getting more boring than ever these days?"

Elizabeth frowned. Her best friend had always annoyed her sister, who resented their intimacy and complained that Enid Rollins was the dullest thing since boiled rice.

"You know I don't think Enid's one bit boring," Elizabeth said quietly. "And you also know it upsets me when you say mean things about her."

Jessica tried to look innocent. "I didn't say anything *mean*," she protested. "I just think she could use a little jazzing up. I mean, that denim thing she was wearing last night at the Beach Disco—"

"Jess," Elizabeth said warningly.

Jessica sighed. "OK, OK. Speaking of the Beach Disco," she said, quickly changing the subject, "you and Guy Chesney sure spent a lot of time together. What's going on?" She grabbed an orange from the fruit bowl and began to peel it. "You're not starting to like him, are you?"

Elizabeth's eyebrows shot up. "Guy Chesney?

94

No," she replied. "I mean, not the way you're implying. He was trying to find out if I knew anything about the mystery singer."

"See?" Jessica shrieked. "Everyone thinks you know something. Liz, if you're holding out on your very own twin . . ."

"I'm not," Elizabeth assured her, getting up from the table and putting her dishes in the sink. "You'd be the first to know, Jess. By the way," she added, turning the hot water on, "how are you planning to get the rocking chair into the Fiat? It'll never fit."

"I guess I'll have to call someone with a big car," Jessica said. She snapped her fingers, looking triumphant. "Max Dellon's van!" she exclaimed. "I'll call him right now."

Elizabeth laughed. This looked to her like a good time to make a hasty exit.

Twenty minutes later Elizabeth had parked the Fiat outside the Music Center and was hurrying into the brightly lit store. The Music Center consisted of three rooms: a record and cassette room, a showroom for musical instruments and sheet music, and a small studio for lessons. Row after row of albums filled the bins set up in the main room, and Elizabeth began thumbing through the albums under *H* in the Rhythm & Blues section.

"Here it is," Elizabeth said to herself, taking the album out and glancing up at the cash regis-

95

ter. The salesperson was busy with another customer. Rather than wait in the main room Elizabeth wandered next door, letting her eye run over the gorgeous instruments. She had never played anything herself, but she loved music, and it was a pleasure to see such beautiful equipment so nicely displayed.

Elizabeth was just picking up a piece of sheet music when she heard a guitar playing in the small back room. She was too far away to hear well, but whoever it was sounded good. Putting the sheet music back, Elizabeth walked toward the half-closed door of the studio.

"See, you put your fingers here," she heard a clear female voice saying. "No. Like *this*. See?"

The voice sounded oddly familiar, but Elizabeth couldn't place it.

"Play that song again," a child's voice urged, and the girl laughed.

"OK, just once more, and then *you* have to play it. OK?"

"OK," the child said. Elizabeth was just outside the studio now, but she still couldn't see inside. She knew she shouldn't be eavesdropping on *a lesson*, but she felt strangely drawn to the girl's voice. Why did it sound so familiar? she wondered.

The next minute the girl strummed her guitar, picked out a chord or two, and began to sing.

"He's everything in the world to me
He makes me feel, he's teaching me to see
. . .
I'm telling you, my world is turning over.
The storms are gone, and morning's coming
up
All sun and four-leaf clover . . ."

Elizabeth felt a prickling sensation on the back of her neck. That voice, that rich, throaty voice! It was so powerful and distinctive that she'd know it anywhere!

It was the anonymous songwriter—the girl who had sung and written the wonderful song, "Outside, Looking In."

Her heart pounding, Elizabeth moved forward into the doorway of the studio. The girl was bent over her guitar, her fuzzy brown hair hanging over her face. At first Elizabeth couldn't see who she was. But the next minute the girl looked up and stared straight at Elizabeth, her mouth dropping open and the song dying on her lips.

"Lynne," Elizabeth said, too surprised even to move.

The color drained from Lynne's face. "Johnny," she said to the little boy who was sitting next to her, his own guitar almost as big as he was. "Wait here for a sec, OK? I have to talk to someone for a minute."

"Lynne," Elizabeth repeated, amazed. "I can't

97

believe it! You're the one who wrote 'Outside, Looking In'! You're the anonymous songwriter!" Just then Elizabeth remembered bumping into Lynne in the doorway of the *Oracle* office. Everything came together at once.

"Shhh," Lynne said. There was a desperate expression in her eyes.

Elizabeth regarded her closely. Lynne looked different, but she couldn't figure out why. Her eyes! she realized with a start. She wasn't wearing her glasses.

"You mustn't tell a soul, Liz," the girl said passionately, putting her hand beseechingly on Elizabeth's arm. "I'm serious. I'd die if anyone found out. Promise you won't tell?"

Elizabeth's mouth dropped open. "But you're so talented. Why don't you want people to know it's you? Don't you want credit for writing that fabulous song?"

Lynne reddened. "You really like it?"

"It's terrific!" Elizabeth said. "Lynne, you are *so* talented! Don't you realize," she added, dropping her voice, "how excited you've made everyone who's heard it? The Droids are just desperate to find you. They want to tell you how great you are. And they want you to sing your song in public!"

Lynne stared at her. "You're kidding," she said, stricken. "I wouldn't do that in a million years. Don't you understand, Liz? That's why I didn't put my name on the song. I'd never be able to perform in front of other people."

Elizabeth looked closely at the agitated girl. "Guy Chesney is the one who's *really* bent on finding you," she remarked. "In fact, he's pretty close to getting frantic about the whole thing. I've never seen anyone so eager to find a girl!"

Lynne paled. "That's"—she cleared her throat—"that's part of the reason I don't want him to find out it's only me," she murmured, not looking at Elizabeth.

"Why?" Elizabeth demanded. "What on earth are you talking about?"

Lynne shrugged, obviously embarrassed. "I feel like I can tell you this," she said softly, "even though it makes me feel like a total moron. But look at me, Liz! Nobody knows me at school. I'm the girl whose name no one can remember, the tall, skinny girl no one ever wants to dance with. So how's Guy going to feel when his fantasy songwriter turns out to be no one other than Lynne Henry?" Her eyes filled with tears. "It would break his heart," she said passionately. "And I wouldn't do that to Guy. Not the way I—" Her voice broke off, and she looked away.

Elizabeth wondered what the rest of her sentence might have been. *"Not the way I feel about him,"* she thought. She remembered the words of Lynne's beautiful song. "Day after day it's

99

him and him only." Could that "him" possibly be Guy Chesney?

"Lynne," Elizabeth said in a low voice, "this may not be any of my business. I don't know you very well. Maybe you're shy, and maybe sometimes you feel awkward about yourself, but don't you think everyone has felt that?"

Lynne stared reproachfully at Elizabeth. "Not *you*," she said enviously. "God, I'd do anything in the world to be you! I'll bet you've never felt self-conscious in your whole life."

"That's crazy," Elizabeth said. "I wouldn't be human if I didn't feel self-conscious sometimes! You just can't let it get to you. You have to think about the things that make you special. For instance," she added, "would you want to be me, even if you knew that I can't sing a note? That I've never played a musical instrument and that I couldn't write a song like yours if someone had a gun to my head?"

Lynne stared at her. "You—are you sure? You really couldn't?"

Elizabeth laughed. "My music teacher from junior high said I was a disaster."

"I guess I'd miss being able to play guitar," Lynne admitted. "Maybe I take music for granted."

Elizabeth shrugged. "Maybe that means you take *more* than music for granted, too. That can't be the only thing about you that's special." She looked speculatively at the girl. "Guy heard something in that song that struck him as unique—something he wants desperately to find. Why can't you give him a chance?"

"He told me . . ." Lynne was getting choked up. She fought hard for control. "Because he told me once that Linda Ronstadt was his dream singer. He went on and on about her. I'm sure he imagines the girl who sings 'Outside, Looking In' looks just like Linda Ronstadt—or better. I can't disappoint him."

"Well, it's up to you," Elizabeth said. "But I don't know how long your secret will last. Guy is really determined to find out the truth."

Lynne looked away uneasily. "Just promise me you won't tell anyone," she begged. "I mean it, Liz. I just couldn't bear it. It would kill me."

Elizabeth sighed. "OK," she said at last. "I promise."

But she felt terrible about it. Driving home, she kept remembering the look on Guy's face the night before, as he stood on the beach and stared out at the sea.

Elizabeth couldn't help feeling that Lynne wasn't even giving herself a chance. It might be the very best thing that could happen to the girl. Obviously Lynne was insecure. But it wasn't doing her any good to hide behind her shell, avoiding any attempt to change.

If Guy found out somehow . . .

But she had promised. And if there was one thing that Elizabeth Wakefield took seriously, it was a promise. It looked as if Guy Chesney's mystery singer was going to remain a mystery for good.

"This is so much fun!" Enid cried. It was eight-thirty on Saturday night, and the Rock Around the Clock evening in the school gym was off to a roaring start. The gym looked fabulous. The cheerleaders had decorated the walls with fifties posters, college banners, and silly cutouts of rocking chairs. The lights were dim, and The Droids were playing up on a large platform at one end of the gym. Their first song had been, of course, "Rock Around the Clock," and next to them, in an oval spotlight, Jessica was rocking back and forth in the rocker she had brought over in The Droid's van.

"I can't believe how silly it is." Elizabeth giggled. Actually she was impressed with how smoothly everything was going. Most of her friends had dressed up in fifties' style clothing. Winston had his hair greased back and was wearing a polka-dot bow tie, black loafers, jeans, and a white shirt. Other boys were wearing dark sunglasses, chinos or Bermuda shorts, plaid shirts, and white socks. The girls wore circle skirts, bobby socks, saddle shoes, and cardigans buttoned up the back. Jessica, who apparently loved being literally in the spotlight, had dug up an old skirt that actually had a poodle on the front of it in a thrift shop. Her blond hair was pulled back in a high ponytail and tied with a ribbon. Elizabeth was wearing black slacks that ended midcalf and a sleeveless white blouse.

Lynne Henry, she noticed, had *not* shown up. Elizabeth hadn't expected her to. From what she knew about Lynne, school dances weren't really her thing. All the same, Elizabeth couldn't get the girl off her mind. Every time she glanced at Guy playing on stage, she felt a lump in her throat. If only she could tell him!

As if he had been reading her mind, Guy stepped up to the microphone. He was wearing jeans and a white T-shirt rolled up at the sleeves. His slicked-back hair and dark glasses completed the look.

"I hope you're all having fun," Guy said into the mike, and the crowd screamed and cheered for several minutes before he could get their attention again. "We have a special song we want to play now," Guy said, his voice serious. "Written by a very special young woman—whoever and wherever she is. The song is called 'Outside, Looking In,' and tonight it will be sung by our very own Dana Larson." More cheers greeted this news.

"And I'd like to dedicate it," Guy added, scanning the crowd seriously, "to the girl who wrote it." This really broke the crowd up, and Elizabeth could barely hear the first few bars of the song.

Her eyes stung with tears as she heard Dana's rich, pretty voice singing Lynne's song. "Day after day I'm feeling kind of lonely. . . . Day after day it's him and him only. . . ."

The look on Guy's face as Dana sang said it all. He was so moved Elizabeth was almost afraid he'd cry.

The melody floated hauntingly around the gym. People swayed to the music, holding each other tenderly. It was a song to fall in love to, Elizabeth thought.

And looking at Guy's face, she had a feeling it was also a song to fall in love *with*.

She wondered where Lynne Henry was just then. Was she feeling lonely? Was she wishing she could hold that special someone? It looked to Elizabeth as though Guy Chesney was feeling exactly the same way. And she was more certain than ever that Guy was the one Lynne Henry had been dreaming of for so many lonely days and nights.

Ten

Lynne was sitting upstairs in her bedroom on Saturday evening, her hairbrush in her hand. Everyone else at school was at the dance, she thought, and she was sitting here alone. She wondered what Guy was doing. Was he playing with The Droids? Were they playing—she felt tears prick behind her eyelids—her song?

Lynne took a deep breath. She had been doing nothing but thinking since that morning, since her run-in with Elizabeth Wakefield, and she felt as if she had come to some kind of turning point. For the last few days, Lynne had felt more vulnerable than ever before, listening to the advice people gave her and the things they said to her with a new sensitivity. She still couldn't believe Elizabeth had overheard her singing that morning. Of all the rotten luck!

But Lynne had taken Elizabeth's words to heart. And she had been thinking about little else since. Was it possible that Guy was really looking for *her*? That her song had affected him so strongly?

Remember Linda Ronstadt, she told herself. *Remember the way Guy's face looked when he talked about singers he liked.* Lynne couldn't believe he would ever like *her*. Oh, she knew he liked her as a friend. He'd been really nice to her. He had offered her a ride to the softball game, and he always looked happy when he ran into her at school. But *liking* her as a girlfriend—ha! That would never happen in a million years.

Still . . . Lynne had made a decision the night before, and she was going to go through with it. She had decided she was sick and tired of looking unkempt. She really wanted to try her hardest to take care of herself. She could already see an improvement, just from wearing the contact lenses and taking pains with her clothing. And that night—her mother had promised to do her hair for her and show her how to use makeup!

"Lynne? Are you ready?" her mother asked, knocking on the door.

"Ready, Mom," Lynne said, bouncing to her feet. She couldn't believe how much nicer it was to be with her mother now. They were actually having fun together.

Ten minutes later her mother was towel-drying Lynne's hair, frowning at her daughter's reflection in the big mirror in her bathroom. "I think you need to take advantage of the wave in your hair without letting it get unruly," she mused, lifting Lynne's hair away from her head. "Actually, you have really nice hair, sweetheart. It just needs to be blown dry, I think. And trimmed a little. We could do a lot here!"

Lynne laughed. "I feel sort of like a guinea pig," she confided. "Do you think it's always scary for people, getting made over?"

"Of course it is," her mother told her. "It makes you feel really vulnerable, as though you have your whole self on the line, or something."

While her mother combed out her hair, Lynne sat very still. She had loved having her hair brushed when she was a little girl.

"What's everyone else at school up to tonight?" her mother asked casually. "Isn't there some kind of dance at school? I saw Mrs. Matthews at the salon today, and she said her son was going to something at the gym."

Lynne frowned. "There's a dance, but I didn't feel like going."

Her mother didn't comment, and suddenly Lynne felt like telling her the whole story about the song. It came out in fits and starts, and her mother listened quietly, not interrupting at all.

"How wonderful," she said when Lynne was

finally through. "I'm so proud of you, sweetie. I'd love to hear your song!"

Lynne reddened. "You mean you don't think I'm a total goon for turning it in without my name on it?"

"Of course not! I understand," her mother told her. "It's hard telling the world how you feel. You know," she added thoughtfully, "your father would be so proud of you if he knew about your music. He always wanted to write songs, too. But I don't think he really had the courage. I think he was almost afraid of taking the risk—of baring his soul."

Lynne was shocked. Her mother never talked about her father! She felt really special, as if her mother were taking her into her confidence. "Was Daddy really talented?" she asked.

Mrs. Henry looked thoughtful. "He was definitely talented, but he was also afraid of succeeding. He was a terribly frightened man, and success takes a lot of courage."

Lynne stared at her mother. "I want to succeed," she said, swallowing hard. "That's why I want your help, Mom. I want to learn to be braver somehow."

Her mother hugged her. "I have a feeling," she said softly, "that you're going to make it."

"I hope so," Lynne said, her eyes shining with tears.

As Mrs. Henry picked up her blow dryer and

hairbrush, she smiled fondly at Lynne in the mirror. "So tell me," she said conversationally, turning the blow dryer on low; "a little bit about this Guy Chesney."

"Liz!" Guy called, hurrying across the crowded dance floor. "I've been hoping I'd get a chance to talk to you tonight."

The Droids were taking a much needed break, letting the cheerleaders provide entertainment for fifteen or twenty minutes.

"You guys are wonderful," Elizabeth said warmly. "I really loved 'Outside, Looking In.' It sounded superb with back-up music!"

"Yes," Guy said moodily, "but it's nowhere near as good as it would be if we had the real singer doing it."

"Don't let Dana hear you saying that," Elizabeth said lightly.

"Don't get me wrong. Dana's the best. It's just that that song is so special. And the mystery woman sings it so beautifully."

"I know," Elizabeth said, trying to avoid his gaze. She was afraid he would realize she knew the singer's identity the minute he looked into her eyes. She felt as if her secret was written all over her face.

"Liz," Guy said suddenly, "I'm going out of my mind. I just can't stand it anymore. I feel like

I've got to find out who she is. I want to run an ad in *The Oracle*. Will you help me write it?"

Elizabeth shook her head. "You've got to stop looking for her, Guy," she told him.

"What? Are you kidding?"

"No," Elizabeth said. "I'm not. Guy, what would you say if I told you that she doesn't want to be found out?"

Guy's eyes widened. "You know something!" he exclaimed, grabbing her by the arm. "Liz, what's going on? Did you hear something? Did someone tell you—"

"I can't tell you," Elizabeth said, feeling awful. He looked so distraught, and she really wanted to help him, especially since it was so clear to her that morning how anguished Lynne was about keeping her identity a secret. But she felt she couldn't go back on her word.

"Let's go outside," Guy said, looking around in confusion at the crowds of students laughing and talking in the darkened gym. "I've got to talk to you, Liz. I feel like I'm going nuts or something. You're the only person I can talk to."

"All right," Elizabeth said, sighing. "But I don't think I'm going to be able to help you very much."

It was cool outside, and the quiet was a nice change. Elizabeth sat down next to Guy on the grassy slope in front of the school and looked up at the silvery moon. *What a beautiful night*, she thought.

"Liz," Guy said, his voice low and urgent, "I don't know what's going on with me. These past two days . . . I don't know, I've been acting like a crazy person. I can't sleep, I'm not hungry, I'm—"

"In love," Elizabeth said, smiling at him. "Sounds like all the symptoms, Guy."

"In love?" Guy stared at her, his eyebrows lifted. A minute later, toying with a blade of grass, Guy smiled sheepishly. "Yeah, I guess I am," he said incredulously. "But tell me that's normal—falling in love with a voice on a tape! That's about the dumbest thing I've ever heard of."

"Not if the voice is *that* voice," Elizabeth said feelingly.

"But what am I supposed to do about it?" He sat up straighter and ran his fingers through his hair, then frowned at the greasy stuff that came off on his fingers. "I can't believe people actually used this stuff on their hair all the time," he said, wiping it on the lawn. "Liz, I'm a wreck. You've got to help me!"

Elizabeth took a deep breath. "I want to help you," she said softly. "But the girl, the mystery songwriter, I mean, made me promise not tell anyone who she is. And I just can't go back on my word, Guy. I'd feel too terrible."

111

"You mean you actually saw her?" Guy leaned forward, his face lighting up. "God, Liz, I can't believe she even exists! It's like—" He looked away, his voice choking up. "That song. It's like she's singing right to me. You know what I mean?"

"Yes," Elizabeth said, looking away. "I do."

"I just can't imagine actually *seeing* her. It seems so hard to imagine now. Is she a junior? Do I know her?"

"I really can't tell you," she repeated stubbornly. "But, yes, I think you know her," she added guiltily, wondering if it was fair to divulge even that much.

"Tell me one thing," Guy said urgently. "I have to hurry, Liz. We've got to start playing again in a few minutes. But I just want to know this. Why doesn't she want anyone to know who she is?"

Elizabeth thought hard. She wasn't sure what to say. How could she repeat what Lynne had told her without giving away her secret?

"She's shy," she said falteringly, thinking fast. "I think she's worried about exposure. And also . . ." her voice trailed off.

"And also, what?"

"Well, I think she's self-conscious about her appearance. She thinks people have certain expectations about the way performers should look. And she doesn't feel that she lives up to those standards. She thinks . . . well, that people are expecting Linda Ronstadt, or something. And they'll be disappointed when that isn't who turns up."

Guy stared at her. "Linda Ronstadt . . ." he repeated, as if the name struck him for some reason. Suddenly he jumped to his feet. "Did she say that? Did she mention Linda Ronstadt?"

"Yes," Elizabeth said, amazed by his reaction. "But why should that—"

"Elizabeth," Guy said, "you've saved my life!" He let out a whoop and began jumping up and down on the lawn. "I don't know how to thank you!"

Elizabeth stared after him. What had she said? He acted as if—well, as if she'd somehow told him who the mystery singer was. But she had absolutely no idea how that was possible.

Eleven

"Well, what do you think?" Mrs. Henry asked, swiveling Lynne around in the chair upstairs at the Silver Door. "I think the eye shadow really brings out the gold in your eyes." It was Sunday afternoon, and the place was empty—the perfect time, as her mother had put it, for experimenting. And experiment they had! Lynne couldn't believe what she'd been through. Sauna, manicure, exercises, makeup, and skin-care lessons.

"It looks wonderful, Mom," Lynne said gratefully, a lump in her throat. She couldn't believe how eager her mother was to help her. For years Lynne had been such a brat, refusing to confide in her mother, acting hostile and difficult. All of that had changed now, and it made Lynne's heart ache to see how easy it was to bridge the gap between them. Her mother had been ready and waiting—the estrangement had all been *her* fault.

Her mother sighed. "I wish it was as easy to make you feel wonderful *inside*," she mused. "As far as looks go, you look like a different person! But"—she paused meaningfully—"do you feel any better about yourself? That's what really matters, you know."

"I know," Lynne said gravely, holding her head up high as she inspected her makeup in the mirror. "And to be totally truthful, Mom, I just don't know yet. I know I want to try, though," she added. "That's something isn't it?"

Her mother hugged her impulsively. "That's the most important thing of all."

Lynne sneaked another look at herself. Her mother was right; she did look like a different person. She was wearing a red T-shirt dress tied with a wide cotton sash below her waist. The dress came down to her knees, a good length for someone of her height, according to Mrs. Henry. Lynne had to admit the overall look was superb. She looked curvier than usual in the bright, soft dress. It was as comfortable as her old sweatshirt and jeans, but it made her look so elegant, so sophisticated! Her hair curled softly around her face, and, with makeup and without glasses her eyes seemed enormous. She looked—well, she hated to admit it—pretty good. Not gorgeous, but interesting. Not a face she could imagine on an album cover . . .

Still, it was one thing to feel self-confident here, in the deserted salon, with her mother behind her. Facing the kids at school the following day looking like this was going to be a whole other story. Lynne felt nervous every time she thought about confessing that she was the one who had written "Outside, Looking In." Somehow she just couldn't imagine it. The old Lynne Henry had written that song. Why couldn't she just let the secret stay a secret? She'd write another song, one with her own name on it, in a few weeks, a few months. . . .

She still wasn't ready to take responsibility for the song that had won Guy Chesney's heart.

Lynne's heart beat faster, thinking about Guy. What would he think of her new look? Would he laugh at her for trying to improve her appearance? She couldn't imagine he would be that unkind, but she was nervous all the same.

And the next day, she remembered uneasily, The Droids were going to announce who the winner of the song contest was. Would her song have a chance if she didn't reveal her identity? Or would they disqualify it?

Lynne really wanted the song to win, even though she hadn't been willing to play by the rules. But she loved "Outside, Looking In." It would always be special for her. And she wanted The Droids to feel the same way about it.

"Hey," her mother was saying, a puzzled smile on her pretty face, "I was asking if you want to stop somewhere and get a salad or something for dinner before we go home. Are you hungry?"

Lynne forced a smile. "Mom, thank you so much for everything," she said, jumping up and giving her a warm hug. "I look so much better. It's like a dream come true! And, yes, I'd love to get something to eat," she concluded, flashing her mother a look of gratitude.

The least she could do was keep her mother company while she ate. She couldn't tell her that she wasn't hungry and that her stomach felt as though it was doing flip-flops. Until she saw Guy again, she had a feeling the butterflies in her stomach just weren't going to go away!

Lynne was about to step outside Monday morning when the telephone rang. "Darn," she said aloud. She didn't want to be late, and she had taken so long getting dressed that she was already five minutes behind schedule. But she knew the final effect was worth it. She was wearing a pair of sleek black jeans, a white T-shirt, and a crayon-bright cotton vest. Flat black espadrilles completed the look, and didn't add any inches to her height, either. For the first time in her life, Lynne had enjoyed getting dressed. Adding the final touches, black earrings and some careful, subtle makeup, had taken almost as long as eating breakfast. But it was fun! And she knew she looked good.

"Lynne, will you get that?" her mother called from upstairs.

"Sure!" Lynne called back, hurrying to the phone. She got it on the fourth ring.

"Hi," a low, friendly voice said on the other line. "Is Lynne there, please?"

"This is Lynne," she replied, thinking, *Who on earth is this?*

"Lynne, this is Guy Chesney."

Lynne almost dropped the receiver. But the "new" Lynne Henry took over. "Oh, hi," she said, just the right combination of surprise and casual curiosity in her voice. "What's up? I was just on my way out the door."

"That's why I'm calling," he told her. "I'm on my way out, too, and I wondered if we could walk together."

Lynne thought her heart was going to stop beating. She couldn't believe her ears. Guy Chesney was calling *her* to ask if she wanted to walk with him! The old Lynne Henry was collapsing with disbelief and excitement. But the new Lynne Henry, thank heavens, was saying with perfect poise, "That would be really nice.

Why don't I meet you at the corner in a few minutes?"

"Great!" Guy said.

Lynne stared at the receiver before she hung up. She couldn't believe it. Was it possible Guy actually liked her company? That he actually wanted to be with her?

Don't get out of control, the old Lynne warned. *He just wants to walk to school with you. It's not exactly a date!*

Lynne stuck her chin out stubbornly. Still, it was a start. She practically floated to the corner, unable to squelch the feeling of joy that was flooding through her. Guy was already waiting when she reached the corner.

"Hi," he said, looking quizzically at her as if he were trying to figure out what was different about her. "Hey, you look terrific!" he exclaimed. "I never knew you had such pretty eyes behind those glasses of yours."

Lynne smiled, speechless.

The two walked in silence for a while—an easy, comfortable silence, punctuated now and then by Guy's cheerful whistling.

"You sure seem happy today," Lynne remarked, looking closely at him. "What's going on?"

"Well, you know The Droids are announcing the winner of the songwriting contest today at lunchtime," he reminded her. "I'm just happy because we found such a terrific song. It'll really be fabulous to announce the winner."

"Really?" Lynne's mouth felt dry. "Who's the winner?" she asked, trying to sound casual.

"Oh, there really wasn't any question from the beginning," Guy told her, smiling. "I mean, right from the first we knew we had one song that was far better than anything else anyone our age could do. In fact, I was so excited about it that I wrote an arrangement for it and we played it Saturday night—although we didn't announce that it was the winning song, of course."

"Which song?" Lynne repeated faintly.

" 'Outside, Looking In,' of course," Guy said reproachfully. "You heard it on my Walkman, remember?"

"Yes," Lynne whispered.

"Well?" Guy demanded. "Isn't it superb? Can you possibly imagine a better entry?"

Lynne didn't say anything for a minute. "But you don't know who wrote the song," she protested, her heart pounding wildly. "What are you going to do about that?"

"The mystery is solved," Guy said lightly, looking as though he were enjoying himself immensely.

Lynne stared at him. "What—what do you mean?"

"Well," he told her, "my dad has a friend who's a terrific artist—a guy named Charlie Porter. He's a police artist. He draws those pictures they use in police stations and on the news. You know, pictures drawn just from someone's description."

Lynne felt a sudden wave of relief. For a minute she'd been afraid Elizabeth had blown her cover. But it didn't sound as though Guy was on to anything at all.

"Anyway," he went on, "last night I played the tape for Charlie. I've heard it so many times, and I've thought about the singer so much that I was able to describe her to him perfectly. Every detail—the hair, the eyes . . ."

"Can I see the picture?" Lynne asked, a lump forming in her throat. She knew it was ridiculous, but she was beginning to feel jealous of this anonymous singer. Guy was in love with a phantom! If only he knew . . .

"Nope," Guy said, smiling fondly at her. "That's part of the surprise. Elizabeth Wakefield is helping me photocopy a flyer that we're going to distribute at lunch today. It's an exclusive story on the mystery songwriter, and we're going to print the picture with the story. You can see it then," he concluded, looking delighted with his plan.

Lynne felt distinctly peculiar. "You're pretty crazy about this singer, aren't you?" she asked carefully, surprised by her own boldness.

Guy looked straight at her, his face suddenly

122

serious. "Yes," he said, taking a deep breath. "I think I'm falling in love with her. Does that sound crazy to you?"

"No," Lynne said dully. It didn't sound crazy. No crazier than anything else these days.

She couldn't believe it. And it was all her fault. If she'd had the courage to put her name on her own song, this never would have happened. Now she had a secret rival, only the rival didn't exist!

Lynne was sure she would be humiliated at lunchtime. Guy had no doubt described the girl of his dreams to this artist. Someone sultry, beautiful, unattainably perfect—someone who looked like Linda Ronstadt.

And that beautiful girl's picture was going to be printed above the lyrics to *her* song!

Lynne couldn't believe the morning was finally over. It felt as if it had been days since she had said goodbye to Guy in front of the drinking fountain in the main hall before homeroom. Her classes had dragged interminably. All she could think about was lunchtime and the flyer with the imaginary girl's portrait plastered all over it. Not only that, but every single person she ran into had a comment about her "new look." It made Lynne feel shaky and scared, knowing everyone had noticed her appearance.

Well, lunchtime was finally there. Lynne was

glad it was all going to be over with at last. She had made a mistake, not taking credit for her own work from the beginning, and she was paying for it now, paying for it every time she saw the look on Guy's face and realized he was really in love with this nonexistent girl. But she'd learned her lesson.

"Lynne!" a low voice exclaimed at her side.

It was Elizabeth Wakefield, her face curious and sympathetic at the same time.

"Hi, Liz," Lynne said, opening her locker with trembling fingers. "I hear you're distributing a flyer with a drawing of the mystery singer at lunchtime."

"Yes," Elizabeth said, "but how did—"

"Liz!" Guy called from down the hall. "Come on! I need your help passing these things around."

Elizabeth sighed. "I'll talk to you later," she said apologetically, moving away from her. "But, Lynne, how did he know?" she called from several feet away, a perplexed expression on her face.

"How did—" Lynne stared after her. How did he know what? What was she talking about?

Head lowered, Lynne headed toward the cafeteria. She had forgotten all about how different she looked. The old Lynne Henry was back in control. She felt awkward, oversized, clumsy—and very much alone.

Counting the change in her hand, she moved blindly into the lunch line, oblivious to what was going on. The next thing she knew, people were crowding around her, saying a million things at once: "Congratulations!" "How'd you do it?" "When did you start writing songs?"

She couldn't believe her ears. "What are you talking about?" she cried as Caroline Pearce patted her on the back. "What song? What are you saying?"

"Look at this!" Winston exclaimed, passing her a single sheet of paper.

Lynne's breath caught in her throat. "Mystery Songwriter Wins Contest!" the headline ran. And underneath, over a beautifully printed copy of her song, was an artist's careful rendering of her own face.

There was no denying it. Guy had described the singer to his friend Charlie in perfect detail—the soft, slightly unruly hair; the large, almond-shaped eyes; the stubborn chin; the expression halfway between dreaminess and laughter. It was her own face. Not the old Lynne Henry, but the way she imagined herself if she closed her eyes and tried to conjure up her own image.

Lynne felt suddenly dizzy. She couldn't even begin to figure out how Guy had guessed she had written the song. She was too affected by the exclamations from her classmates. She couldn't even stay in the lunch line, the crowd around her was so persistent. "Lynne! Lynne!" they kept chanting as though she was some kind of star or something.

As though she was a Somebody.

Suddenly Lynne focused on one face in the crowd. It was Guy, and he was looking at her as if . . .

His words came back to her in a rush. "I think I'm falling in love with her." And he'd known she had written the song! Could he really mean it? Could he really mean that he was starting to fall in love with *her*?

"Lynne!" Guy called, his voice choking with emotion. A minute later he had fought his way through the crowd and grabbed her by the arm. "The Droids want to know if you'll sing your song right now. The office has given us permission to use the mike in here, and I'll play guitar to back you up."

Lynne stared at him, her eyes swimming with tears. "How did you know?" she demanded, her voice low.

"I'll tell you later," he said, smiling down at her. Suddenly he grabbed her hand, lacing her fingers with his own. "Will you sing for us? Say you will, Lynne. *Please*."

"OK," Lynne said, looking deep into his eyes.

A few minutes later she was up in front of the whole cafeteria, the mike in her hand and Guy behind her. Dana Larson had introduced her, and the entire cafeteria had burst into applause and cheers.

Lynne took a deep breath and turned to look at Guy. His reassuring smile was all she needed. She knew she would sing better than she had in her whole life.

"Day after day, I'm feeling kind of lonely," she sang, her voice rich and true. She saw Elizabeth Wakefield in the audience, smiling proudly at her, and at the back of the room, Mr. Collins was listening, an incredulous smile on his face. Lynne knew she was singing well. She had tears in her eyes because it was her song to Guy, and he knew it. Every word came from her heart.

She barely heard the roar of applause that greeted the last word of the song. Guy was grabbing her hand. "Let's get out of here," he said gruffly, and she followed him out the door, running next to him onto the patio, which was usually crowded with students eating lunch. That day, however, everyone had rushed inside to hear the song, and so the patio was empty. Lynne remembered the daydream she'd had time after time. There she was, her hand in his . . .

And the next thing she knew, Guy was taking her in his arms, kissing her as if he hoped the moment would never end.

"Oh, Guy!" Lynne gasped, staring wonderingly at him. It was every bit as magical as she had dreamed. She wished there was some way to explain to him how incredible it was to discover that real life could be even more perfect than her fantasy had been. But from the look in his eyes, she had a feeling she didn't have to explain.

"I love you," Guy said wonderingly, cupping her chin with his hand. And she knew he was feeling the same way she was.

They had each woken up from a dream. And they had each found out that that was where real happiness began—right there in the real world, in each other's arms.

Twelve

"Move over, Lila!" Jessica exclaimed, shaking out her enormous striped beach towel next to her friend. A group of kids had decided to head over to the beach that afternoon after school, and Jessica was trying to position her towel so she'd get as much sun as possible on her face.

"I'm half asleep," Lila moaned. "If I move over, I'll wake up from the most delicious dream."

"Well, wake up, then," Jessica said. "You're pigging the best part of the beach."

Lila sat up and dramatically flung one hand across her eyes. "Jessica, you are just *too* childish. How can one part of the beach—"

"Tell me about your dream," Jessica interrupted, plopping down on her towel and reaching for her suntan lotion.

"A mysterious oil magnate was proposing marriage to me on his jet," Lila told her. "He had a diamond ring the size of a hard-boiled egg in his hands."

Jessica laughed. "Sounds more like a nightmare to me, Lila. *I'd* rather dream about your cousin Christopher. When's he coming?"

"I don't know," Lila said, pulling her bathing suit half an inch away from her skin to examine her tan line. "Christopher doesn't confine himself to dates the way some people do." She looked at Jessica with an expression that clearly said that confining oneself to a date was the worst thing in the world.

"Oh," Jessica said, unconvinced.

"But I'm sure it'll be in the next week or two. And when he comes, I'm going to throw the best party Sweet Valley High has ever seen."

Jessica laughed. "I'm sure you will," she said, losing interest in the subject. She noticed a couple strolling down the beach, hand in hand. "What do you think of Lynne Henry and Guy Chesney?" she asked. "It looks like Lynne won more than the song contest with that hit of hers!"

Lila squinted down the beach. "I have to admit she looks a lot better these days. Maybe love is making her more beautiful."

"Maybe," Jessica said thoughtfully. "Guy's cute, don't you think?"

Lila sighed. "Wait," she said, "until you see

Christopher. You won't think *anyone* around here is cute after you get a look at him!"

Jessica was about to protest that it might be *forever* before she got the chance to see Christopher when a whole crowd of girls from Pi Beta Alpha, the sorority Lila and Jessica belonged to, came over to join them. Private conversation was obviously going to have to wait. Jessica was president of the exclusive sorority, which Elizabeth belonged to in name only.

"That relay you guys threw on Saturday was an absolute scream," Lisa Reed exclaimed. Jessica smiled appreciatively at her. Lisa was a sophomore, a black girl with curly, short hair and a stunning figure.

"It *was* fun," she admitted. "And we raised so much money! We're going to have more than enough to buy new uniforms for the whole squad."

"Mind you," Lila said, lifting an eyebrow, "you still have to *collect* the money people pledged. Remember?"

Jessica shrugged "That'll be easy. Don't be such a spoilsport, Lila."

"Who's being a spoilsport?" Enid Rollins asked as she strolled over to join the group, a beach towel over her arm. "Jess, have you seen Liz anywhere? She was supposed to meet me here at three-thirty."

Jessica shook her head. "She said she had to

stop at home to drop something off before coming here. Maybe she got held up."

Enid frowned.

"Speaking of new uniforms," Cara said, "unless we plan on buying one less than we thought, hadn't we better do something about setting up auditions for Helen Bradley's spot?"

Jessica groaned. "I can't bear auditions. It's going to be just awful!"

"Come on, Jess," Cara reproved her. "It's got to be done. And we'd better do it soon, too. I hear the Bradleys may have found a buyer for their house already. That means they might be moving any day now."

"All right, all right," Jessica conceded, watching Enid spread her towel out nearby. For the next few minutes conversation ran from one topic to another—the incredible success of Saturday night's Rock Around the Clock relay; new outfits for the cheerleaders; Lila's cousin Christopher and the upcoming party. At last Lisa mentioned Lynne Henry, and serious speculation began.

"I heard she might audition for some really big band in L.A.," Caroline Pearce said, running sand through her fingers.

"I heard her mother's enrolled her in a six-month make-over program at the Silver Door," Lila Fowler remarked.

"You guys are catty," Enid remarked from

where she sat, a short distance away. "I think she looks great because she's happy. And she's finally gotten recognition for the one thing she loves most in the world—writing music!"

"Looks to me like the thing she loves best in the world is Guy Chesney," Robin Wilson said and laughed. But her laughter was sympathetic. Robin, co-captain of the cheerleading squad, knew what it was like to evolve from an ugly duckling to a swan. Before joining the cheerleading squad, Robin had lost quite a bit of weight—and gained quite a bit of self-confidence. Her heart went out to Lynne, and it was obvious that she was proud of the girl as well as empathetic.

"Well, I think it's magic," Lisa Reed said happily. "Like something in a fairy tale. I just hope someday I find *my* prince the way Lynne Henry has!"

Everyone laughed. "Hey, there's Liz," Enid said suddenly, shading her eyes with her hand. "I wonder why she doesn't have her bathing suit on."

Everyone turned to watch as Elizabeth jogged over to join them, still in the tan chinos and T-shirt she had been wearing at school. "You guys," she was panting as she approached. Dropping down on the sand, she waved a piece of paper at them before she spoke. "You won't believe in a million years what I just found out!"

"What is it?" Jessica asked. "Is everything OK?"

"Oh, yeah," Elizabeth assured her. "More than OK! In fact, I've just gotten wonderful news."

"What is it, Liz?" Cara asked, curious.

Elizabeth looked down at herself and chuckled. "I was in such a hurry to come tell you guys that I didn't even bother to change!" She shook her blond head. "Well, I guess I'd better backtrack first. Do any of you remember Amy Sutton?"

A few of the girls looked perplexed, but Cara, Lila, Caroline, and some of the others remembered her right away. "You mean that girl from middle school?" Caroline asked.

Elizabeth nodded. "She was my very best friend in the sixth grade, remember?"

"That's right!" Lila snapped her fingers. "You two were like—I don't know—bread and butter."

"Peanut butter and jelly," Jessica said.

"You guys!" Elizabeth cried in mock protest. "This is serious! Anyway, Amy moved to Connecticut, remember? Her mother got a fabulous job offer, and the family couldn't pass it up."

"That's right," Jessica said. "I remember how upset you two were then. Connecticut seemed like the other side of the universe."

"Well, it *is* pretty far away," Elizabeth pointed out. "Anyway, after she moved we didn't see much of each other again. I went out to Connecticut once, and she came back here once or twice, but after a year or two we both had found new friends."

Lila frowned. "So what's the deal? Where's Amy now?"

Elizabeth waved the letter at her, her excitement returning. "Well, this is the incredible thing. You know her mother's a sportscaster. Well, the station she's working for in Connecticut is pretty small. And now she's been offered a huge spot on WXAB!"

"You mean the Suttons are moving back to California?" Jessica demanded, clapping her hands. "Liz, that's wonderful!"

"Better yet, they're moving to Sweet Valley. And the really crazy thing is, they've bought the Bradleys' house," Elizabeth told them. "I still can't believe it," she added, shaking her head. "I have to keep pinching myself. I can't believe she'll really be back here again!"

"When are they moving in?" Enid asked, her voice flat.

"Next week," Elizabeth said, smiling warmly at her. "Enid, I can't wait for you to meet Amy! You two are going to love each other."

Enid didn't answer.

"But have you guys been keeping up with

each other all this time?" Cara demanded. "Have you been writing letters?"

Elizabeth shook her head. "Not really. We write at Christmas and on birthdays, but that's all. That's why I was so surprised when I saw her handwriting on the envelope today."

Lila smiled. "Well, with Amy coming back to Sweet Valley and my cousin Christopher visiting any day now, it looks like the next few weeks are going to be pretty exciting."

Elizabeth hugged herself. She was so thrilled about Amy! She couldn't imagine better news. She just couldn't wait for the days to pass until Amy's arrival.

She was far too excited to notice the frown on Enid Rollins's face.

Enid had been Elizabeth's best friend for a long, long time. But obviously not as long as Amy Sutton!

And Enid couldn't help wondering if Elizabeth was going to have any time left for *her* once her former best friend moved into the Bradleys' house the following week.

Will Elizabeth's renewed friendship with Amy Sutton leave Enid stranded? Find out in Sweet Valley High #29, **BITTER RIVALS.**

You're going to love
ON OUR OWN®

Now starring in a brand-new SWEET DREAMS mini-series—Jill and Toni from *Ten Boy Summer* and *The Great Boy Chase*

Is there life after high school? Best friends Jill and Toni are about to find out—on their own.

Jill goes away to school and Toni stays home, but both soon learn that college isn't all fun and games. In their new adventures both must learn to handle new feelings about love and romance.

☐	25723	#1 THE GRADUATES	$2.50
☐	25724	#2: THE TROUBLE WITH TONI	$2.50
☐	25937	#3: OUT OF LOVE	$2.50
☐	26186	#4: OLD FRIENDS, NEW FRIENDS	$2.50
☐	26034	#5: GROWING PAINS	$2.50
☐	26111	#6: BEST FRIENDS FOREVER	$2.50

ON OUR OWN—The books that begin where SWEET DREAMS leaves off.

Prices and availability subject to change without notice.